ORPHEUS
DESCENDING

AND

SUDDENLY LAST
SUMMER

D1124695

BY TENNESSEE WILLIAMS

PLAYS

Camino Real (with *Ten Blocks on the Camino Real*)
Candles to the Sun
Cat on a Hot Tin Roof
Clothes for a Summer Hotel
Fugitive Kind
The Glass Menagerie
A House Not Meant to Stand
A Lovely Sunday for Creve Coeur
The Night of the Iguana
Not About Nightingales
The Notebook of Trigorin

Orpheus Descending & Suddenly Last Summer
The Rose Tattoo (with *The Dog Enchanted by the Divine View*)
Something Cloudy, Something Clear
Spring Storm
Stairs to the Roof
A Streetcar Named Desire
Sweet Bird of Youth (with *The Enemy: Time*)
Baby Doll & Tiger Tail
The Two-Character Play

Vieux Carré

THE THEATRE OF TENNESSEE WILLIAMS

The Theatre of Tennessee Williams, Volume I:
Battle of Angels, A Streetcar Named Desire, The Glass Menagerie

The Theatre of Tennessee Williams, Volume II:
The Eccentricities of a Nightingale, Summer and Smoke, The Rose Tattoo, Camino Real

The Theatre of Tennessee Williams, Volume III:
Cat on a Hot Tin Roof, Orpheus Descending, Suddenly Last Summer

The Theatre of Tennessee Williams, Volume IV:
Sweet Bird of Youth, Period of Adjustment, The Night of the Iguana

The Theatre of Tennessee Williams, Volume V:
The Milk Train Doesn't Stop Here Anymore, Kingdom of Earth (The Seven Descents of Myrtle), Small Craft Warnings, The Two-Character Play (Out Cry)

The Theatre of Tennessee Williams, Volume VI:
27 Wagons Full of Cotton and Other Short Plays
Includes all the plays from the individual volume of 27 *Wagons Full of Cotton and Other Plays* plus *The Unsatisfactory Supper, Steps Must be Gentle, The Demolition Downtown*

The Theatre of Tennessee Williams, Volume VII:
In the Bar of a Tokyo Hotel and Other Plays
Includes all the plays from the individual volume of *Dragon Country* plus *Lifeboat Drill, Now the Cats with Jeweled Claws, This is the Peaceable Kingdom*

The Theatre of Tennessee Williams, Volume VIII:
Vieux Carré, A Lovely Sunday for Creve Coeur, Clothes for a Summer Hotel, The Red Devil Battery Sign

Lois Smith as Carol Cutrere and Cliff Robertson as Valentine Xavier in the original 1957 Broadway production of *Orpheus Descending*.

TENNESSEE WILLIAMS

ORPHEUS DESCENDING

AND

SUDDENLY LAST SUMMER

INTRODUCTIONS BY
MARTIN SHERMAN

A NEW DIRECTIONS BOOK

Manufactured in the United States of America.
New Directions Books are printed on acid-free paper.
Orpheus Descending was first published with *Battle of Angels* in a cloth edition by New Directions in 1958.
Suddenly Last Summer was first published in a cloth edition by New Directions in 1958.
This combination volume was published as New Directions Paperbook 1247 in 2012.
Published simultaneously in Canada by Penguin Canada Books, Ltd.

Library of Congress Cataloging-in-Publication Data
Williams, Tennessee, 1911–1983.
Orpheus descending ; and, Suddenly last summer / Tennessee Williams ; introductions by Martin Sherman.
p. cm.
"A New Directions Book."
Includes bibliographical references and index.
ISBN 978-0-8112-1939-6 (alk. paper)
I. Title. II. Title: Suddenly last summer.
PS3545.I5365O7 2012
812'.54—dc23   2012030255

10 9 8 7 6 5 4 3 2 1

New Directions Books are published for James Laughlin
by New Directions Publishing Corporation
80 Eighth Avenue, New York, NY 10011

CONTENTS

INTRODUCTION TO
ORPHEUS DESCENDING

When Tennessee Williams's *Orpheus Descending* opened on Broadway in March 1957, the esteemed critic of *The New York Times*, Brooks Atkinson, called it "one of Mr. Williams's pleasantest plays." The pleasantries in *Orpheus Descending* include murder, death by blowtorch, convicts eaten alive by dogs, religious fanaticism, hysterical blindness, promiscuity, abortion, lynchings, substance abuse, cancer, prostitution, and arson. In fairness, Atkinson had been watching a tepid production, which he praised, misdirected and miscast, with the blazing exception of a febrile, wraith-like Carol Cutrere played by America's most unheralded great actress, Lois Smith.

Perhaps Atkinson was referring to its themes of love and redemption. For in *Orpheus Descending* there is a genuine merging of souls; two lonely and spiritually intense people find physical and emotional solace in each other, which, except in *The Rose Tattoo*, is an unusual destination in a Williams play. But in *The Rose Tattoo* they have a future; here, in *Orpheus*, a true descent into hell, they are done for. It's as if Williams is saying: If you are sensitive and lucky, you might find someone else sensitive to understand you, but no matter, the world will destroy you anyway. Like most great artists, his was a constant battle between hope and despair. Atkinson found Williams in "a more humane state of mind than he has been in several years." Which of course begs the question, when *wasn't* Tennessee Williams in a humane state of mind? What other playwright has found so much beauty in the most unlikely places?

The unlikely place in *Orpheus Descending* is one of the most venal and corrupt Southern towns ever created, except, of course, it wasn't created: it was an accurate reflection of its time and period. (Atkinson called it "an attractive locale.") I always find it interesting that it is Arthur Miller and not Williams who is labeled the social realist. I doubt that the American theater has ever had a more acute social realist than Tennessee Williams. The confusion is that he was writing realistically about poetic people. When I was very young I spent some time in Louisiana and discovered to my shock that *it was all true*. Williams hadn't made anything up. People talked and behaved the way his characters did. He was virtually reporting. In those days I came upon a burgeoning Blanche DuBois, a Maggie-the-Cat in waiting, Carol Cutrere minus the white makeup, Val Xaviers by the dozen, and innumerable Sister Women and Brother Men, together with hordes of no-neck monsters. I knew, too, a former Southern belle, married to a dentist in New York, who was Amanda Wingfield incarnate. These people all used language in the most gloriously imaginative way.

It is interesting to note that Lady Torrance, a full and vividly created character, is not the person who speaks poetically in *Orpheus*. The great lines in the play, the ones that are often quoted— "we're all of us sentenced to solitary confinement inside our own skins, for life," "there's something wild in the country that only the night people know," "what on earth can you do on this earth but catch at whatever comes near you, with both your hands, until your fingers are broken"—are said by Val and Carol, both South-erners and thus both speaking as they would. Lady is European; her language is more pragmatic—"the show is over, the monkey is dead." Williams was meticulous about the way his characters spoke; often they are Southern and thus often they soar.

My newfound Southern friends were, of course, all outcasts, even poor Phoebe (the Amanda) stuck in the Bronx. Some were from small towns in Mississippi, and once I accompanied a friend back to her former home where the prevailing attitudes were frighteningly similar to the ones in *Orpheus Descending*.

The motivating force in *Orpheus*'s town (curiously unnamed) is racism. Racism is the one word I left out in my list of subject matter above and yet it is probably the most important. Racism drives the play and ultimately destroys all its decent characters. Papa Romano, Lady Torrance's father, is burned to death by the Ku Klux Klan because "he sold liquor to niggers" twenty years before the play begins. That's it. The town fathers are basically not concerned that he sells illegal bootleg whisky or that his little arbor-restaurant features alcoves where unmarried couples can make love. His crime is pure and simple—he treated black men as if they were equals. So they kill him. At the end of the play Lady discovers that her husband, Jabe, led the Klan that fateful night; this discovery leads to her own death (bullet) and that of Val, the guitar-playing itinerant she has taken in (blowtorch). (Atkinson: "a sense of small-town realities.") A single act of racial tolerance and the hatred it sets off have caused the central tragedies of the play.

There are two other characters with wounded souls: Carol Cu-trere, a rich girl who wanders in and out of the town she has been exiled from, and Vee Talbott, the artistic wife of the sheriff. Carol's history is fascinating. She has used up all of her inheritance trying unsuccessfully to put up free clinics for the local black popula-tion in order to stop "the gradual massacre of the colored majority in the county." She then starts a march to the state capital to protest the death sentence of a black man accused, in a case similar to the Scottsboro Boys, of raping a white woman. Except, she only makes it six miles out of town, whereupon she's arrested for lewd vagrancy. This sends Carol, already vulnerable, over the edge—she decides to indeed become a lewd vagrant and thus the damaged creature we meet in the play. The important fact about Carol, often overlooked, is that she was basically a civil rights worker, in a decade before they existed, and pays a terrible price for it. Vee, meanwhile has religious visions because she has been so distressed by the awful things she has witnessed as the wife of a sheriff—blacks beaten and lynched and "runaway convicts torn to pieces by hounds."

All four of these sensitive souls are ruined by the racial hatred that exists around them. It seems to me that *Orpheus Descending* is in fact a play of great political bravery. More so than, for instance, *The Crucible*, unquestionably a brilliant play, but one which nonetheless creates a political metaphor in the distant past to suggest the present. *Orpheus* was written about the times in which it was written. There is no political metaphor. Williams is telling it exactly as it is—or was then—and condemning racial and social attitudes of a large area of America. Williams was often accused in the sixties of being politically silent. But he had already spoken out, years before. No one seemed to notice. Atkinson's review, for instance, never hints that he has witnessed a play with political intent. It has been suggested, not least by Arthur Miller himself, that Williams's work moved the individual and his inner life center stage and that social conditions were symbolized from within the personalities of the characters. That is, of course, partially true, but in *Orpheus Descending*, the inner poetic vision shares the stage with a crusading political conscience.

Just as Carol may seem a creature before her time, so too is Val. This role has often seemed unplayable, and it wasn't until Stuart

Townsend brilliantly embodied him in a production at London's Donmar Warehouse in 2000 that he finally made sense for me. In *Battle Of Angels* (1940), the first version of *Orpheus Descending*, Val was a writer. Townsend took his cue from the original and reimagined Val as a man with a genuine poetic soul. Like many poets, he carries within him a delicate mixture of the genders. Atkinson commended Cliff Robertson's deeply dull performance in the original production as "manly," which may in its day have seemed like an important corrective to Val's gentler side, and indirectly assured us that the character really wasn't gay. But Townsend simply showed us that Val was very much like a creature that was to emerge in America ten years later—a hippie—with an informal attitude toward sex, wandering the countryside with a guitar autographed by Woody Guthrie. How prescient of Williams to write about two young people—Carol and Val—who predicted the concerns and behavior of their counterparts a decade later.

There is another reason to love *Orpheus Descending*. It is a mess. It is disorderly. It wanders. It is itself a lewd vagrant. Characters command the stage, talk to the audience, set the scene, and then disappear for good parts of the play. The ending is old-fashioned melodrama. The central love story is not entirely convincing. It's been rewritten too often. It won't be taught in playwriting class. Well, maybe it should. For the play is the playwright. This, after all, was a disorderly man, and he nakedly puts this on stage. His mind jumps and challenges and taunts and flirts and sometimes flies way off the railway line, but it is always *his* mind. This is, of course, when his mind was still functioning. Some of his later plays are also a mess but not in the same way. Subtle connective tissues are by then missing in the work. What connects all the elements in *Orpheus Descending* is the hyperactive amusement and despair of Williams's racing brain. The less controlled of the great Williams plays have a chaotic purity. A genius is stripping bare, hopping around on burning stones, falling down, jumping up again, but always showing us the goods. Atkinson, in his review, does concede Williams's "magic style of writing" but laments that "he has not ordered his world as decisively as usual." No, and from a scholastic point of view that's a problem. But if you're interested in the messy business of life or art, surely it's a glory.

By the way, Brooks Atkinson has a Broadway theater named after him. Tennessee Williams does not.

MARTIN SHERMAN

ORPHEUS DESCENDING

Orpheus Descending was presented at the Martin Beck Theatre in New York on March 21, 1957, by the Producers Theatre. It was directed by Harold Clurman; the stage set was designed by Boris Aronson, the costumes by Lucinda Ballard, and the lighting by Feder. The cast was as follows:

DOLLY HAMMA	Elizabeth Eustis
BEULAH BINNINGS	Jane Rose
PEE WEE BINNINGS	Warren Kemmerling
DOG HAMMA	David Clarke
CAROL CUTRERE	Lois Smith
EVA TEMPLE	Nell Harrison
SISTER TEMPLE	Mary Farrell
UNCLE PLEASANT	John Marriott
VAL XAVIER	Cliff Robertson
VEE TALBOTT	Joanna Roos
LADY TORRANCE	Maureen Stapleton
JABE TORRANCE	Crahan Denton
SHERIFF TALBOTT	R. G. Armstrong
MR. DUBINSKY	Beau Tilden
WOMAN	Janice Mars
DAVID CUTRERE	Robert Webber
NURSE PORTER	Virgilia Chew
FIRST MAN	Albert Henderson
SECOND MAN	Charles Tyner

Other characters: CONJURE MAN, CLOWN.

ACT ONE

PROLOGUE

Scene: The set represents in nonrealistic fashion a general dry-goods store and part of a connecting "confectionery" in a small Southern town. The ceiling is high and the upper walls are dark, as if streaked with moisture and cobwebbed. A great dusty window upstage offers a view of disturbing emptiness that fades into late dusk. The action of the play occurs during a rainy season, late winter and early spring, and sometimes the window turns opaque but glistening silver with sheets of rain. "TORRANCE MERCANTILE STORE" is lettered on the window in gilt of old-fashioned design.

Merchandise is represented very sparsely and it is not realistic. Bolts of pepperel and percale stand upright on large spools, the black skeleton of a dressmaker's dummy stands meaninglessly against a thin white column, and there is a motionless ceiling fan with strips of flypaper hanging from it.

There are stairs that lead to a landing and disappear above it, and on the landing there is a sinister-looking artificial palm tree in a greenish-brown jardiniere.

But the confectionery, which is seen partly through a wide arched door, is shadowy and poetic as some inner dimension of the play.

Another, much smaller, playing area is a tiny bedroom alcove which is usually masked by an Oriental drapery which is worn dim but bears the formal design of a gold tree with scarlet fruit and fantastic birds.

At the rise of the curtain two youngish middle-aged women, Dolly and Beulah, are laying out a buffet supper on a pair of pink-and-gray-veined marble-topped tables with gracefully curved black-iron legs, brought into the main area from the confectionery. They are wives of small planters and tastelessly overdressed in a somewhat bizarre fashion.

A train whistles in the distance and dogs bark in response from various points and distances. The women pause in their occupations at the tables and rush to the archway, crying out harshly.

DOLLY: Pee Wee!

BEULAH: Dawg!

DOLLY: Cannonball is comin' into th' depot!

BEULAH: You all git down to th' depot an' meet that train!

[*Their husbands slouch through, heavy, red-faced men in clothes that are too tight for them or too loose, and mud-stained boots.*]

PEE WEE: I fed that one-armed bandit a hunnerd nickels an' it coughed up five.

DOG: Must have hed indigestion.

PEE WEE: I'm gonna speak to Jabe about them slots. [*They go out and a motor starts and pauses.*]

DOLLY: I guess Jabe Torrance has got more to worry about than the slot machines and pinball games in that confectionery.

BEULAH: You're not tellin' a lie. I wint to see Dr. Johnny about Dawg's condition. Dawg's got sugar in his urine again, an' as I was leavin' I ast him what was the facks about Jabe Torrance's operation in Mimphis. Well—

DOLLY: What'd he tell you, Beulah?

BEULAH: He said the worse thing a doctor ever can say.

DOLLY: What's that, Beulah?

BEULAH: Nothin' a-tall, not a spoken word did he utter! He just looked at me with those big dark eyes of his and shook his haid like this!

DOLLY [*with doleful satisfaction*]: I guess he signed Jabe Torrance's death warrant with just that single silent motion of his haid.

BEULAH: That's exactly what passed through my mind. I understand that they cut him open— [*Pauses to taste something on the table.*]

DOLLY: —An' sewed him right back up!—that's what I heard . . .

BEULAH: I didn't know these olives had seeds in them!

DOLLY: You thought they was stuffed?

BEULAH: Uh-huh. Where's the Temple sisters?

DOLLY: Where d'you think?

BEULAH: Snoopin' aroun' upstairs. If Lady catches 'em at it she'll give those two old maids a touch of her tongue! She's not a Dago for nothin'!

DOLLY: Ha, ha, no! You spoke a true word, honey . . . [*Looks out door as car passes.*] Well, I was surprised when I wint up myself!

BEULAH: You wint up you'self?

DOLLY: I did and so did you because I seen you, Beulah.

BEULAH: I never said that I didn't. Curiosity is a human instinct.

DOLLY: They got two separate bedrooms which are not even connectin'. At opposite ends of the hall, and everything is so dingy an' dark up there. Y'know what it seemed like to me? A county jail! I swear to goodness it didn't seem to me like a place for white people to live in!—that's the truth . . .

BEULAH [*darkly*]: Well, I wasn't surprised. Jabe Torrance bought that woman.

DOLLY: Bought her?

BEULAH: Yais, he bought her, when she was a girl of eighteen! He bought her and bought her cheap because she'd been thrown over and her heart was broken by that— [*Jerks head toward a passing car, then continues.*] —that Cutrere boy. . . . *Oh,* what a— *Mmmm,* what a—*beautiful* thing he was. . . . And those two met like you struck two stones together and made a fire!—yes—fire . . .

DOLLY: What?

BEULAH: Fire—Ha . . . [*Strikes another match and lights one of the candelabra. Mandolin begins to fade in. The following monologue should be treated frankly as exposition, spoken to audience, almost directly, with a force that commands attention. Dolly does not remain in the playing area, and after the first few sentences, there is no longer any pretense of a duologue*]
—Well, that was a long time ago, before you and Dog moved into Two River County. Although you must have heard of it. Lady's father was a Wop from the old country and when he first come here with a mandolin and a monkey that wore a little green velvet suit, ha ha.
—He picked up dimes and quarters in the saloons—this was before Prohibition. . . .
—People just called him "The Wop," nobody knew his name, just called him "The Wop," ha ha ha. . . .

DOLLY [*off, vaguely*]: Anh-hannnh. . . .

[*Beulah switches in the chair and fixes the audience with her eyes, leaning slightly forward to compel their attention. Her voice is rich with nostalgia, and at a sign of restlessness, she rises and comes straight out to the proscenium, like a pitchman.*

This monologue should set the nonrealistic key for the whole production.]

BEULAH: Oh, my law, well, that was Lady's daddy! Then come Prohibition an' first thing ennyone knew, The Wop had took to bootleggin' like a duck to water! He picked up a piece of land cheap, it was on the no'th shore of Moon Lake which used to be the old channel of the river and people thought some day the river might swing back that way, and so he got it cheap. . . . [*Moves her chair up closer to proscenium.*] He planted an orchard on it; he covered the whole no'th shore of the lake with grapevines and fruit trees, and then he built little arbors, little white wooden arbors with tables and benches to drink in and carry on in, ha ha! And in the spring and the summer, young couples would come out there, like me and Pee Wee, we used to go out there, an' court up a storm, ha ha, just court up a—storm! Ha ha! —The county was dry in those days, I don't mean dry like now, why, now you just walk a couple of feet off the highway and whistle three times like a jay bird and a nigger pops out of a bush with a bottle of corn!

DOLLY: Ain't that the truth? Ha ha.

BEULAH: But in those days the county was dry for true, I mean bone dry except for The Wop's wine garden. So we'd go out to The Wop's an' drink that Dago red wine an' cut up an' carry on an' raise such Cain in those arbors! Why, I remember one Sunday old Doctor Tooker, Methodist minister then, he bust a blood vessel denouncing The Wop in the pulpit!

DOLLY: Lawd have mercy!

BEULAH: Yes, ma'am! —Each of those white wooden arbors had a lamp in it, and one by one, here and there, the lamps would go out as the couples begun to make love . . .

DOLLY: *Oh*—oh . . .

BEULAH: What strange noises you could hear if you listened, calls, cries, whispers, moans—giggles. . . . [*Her voice is soft with recollection.*] —And then, one by one, the lamps would be lighted again, and The Wop and his daughter would sing and play Dago songs. . . . [*Bring up mandolin: voice under "Dicitencello Vuoi."*] But sometimes The Wop would look around for his daughter, and all of a sudden Lady wouldn't be there!

DOLLY: Where would she be?

BEULAH: She'd be with David Cutrere.

DOLLY: Awwwwww—ha ha . . .

BEULAH: —Carol Cutrere's big brother, Lady and him would disappear in the orchard and old Papa Romano, The Wop, would holler, "Lady, Lady!"—no answer whatsoever, no matter how long he called and no matter how loud. . . .

DOLLY: Well, I guess it's hard to shout back, "Here I am, Papa," when where you are is in the arms of your lover!

BEULAH: Well, that spring, no, it was late that summer . . . [*Dolly retires again from the playing area.*] —Papa Romano made a bad mistake. He sold liquor to niggers. The Mystic Crew took action. —They rode out there, one night, with gallons of coal oil—it was a real dry summer—and set that place on fire! —They burned the whole thing up, vines, arbors, fruit trees. —Pee Wee and me, we stood on the dance pavilion across the lake and watched that fire spring up. Inside of tin minutes the whole nawth shore of the lake was a mass of flames, a regular sea of flames, and all the way over the lake we could hear Lady's papa shouting, "Fire, fire, fire!"—as if it was necessary to let people know, and the whole sky lit up with it, as red as Guinea red wine! —Ha ha ha ha. . . . Not a fire engine, not a single engine pulled out of a station that night in Two River County! —The poor old fellow, The Wop, he took a blanket and run up into the orchard to fight the fire single-handed—*and* burned *alive*. . . . Uh-huh! *burned alive*. . . .

[*Mandolin stops short, Dolly has returned to the table to have her coffee.*]

You know what I sometimes wonder?

DOLLY: No. What do you wonder?

BEULAH: I wonder sometimes if Lady has any suspicion that her husband, Jabe Torrance, was the leader of the Mystic Crew the night they burned up her father in his wine garden on Moon Lake?

DOLLY: Beulah Binnings, you make my blood run cold with such a thought! How could she live in marriage twenty years with a man if she knew he'd burned her father up in his wine garden?

[*Dog bays in distance.*]

BEULAH: She could live with him in hate. People can live together in hate for a long time, Dolly. Notice their passion for money. I've always noticed when couples don't love each other they develop a passion for money. Haven't you seen that happen? Of course you have. Now there's not many couples that stay devoted forever. Why, some git so they just barely tolerate each other's existence. Isn't that true?

DOLLY: You couldn't of spoken a truer word if you read it out loud from the Bible!

BEULAH: Barely tolerate each other's existence, and some don't even do that. You know, Dolly Hamma, I don't think half as many married min have committed suicide in this county as the coroner says has done so!

DOLLY: [*with voluptuous appreciation of Beulah's wit*]: You think it's their wives that give them the deep six, honey?

BEULAH: I don't think so, I know so. Why there's couples that loathe and despise the sight, smell and sound of each other before that round-trip honeymoon ticket is punched at both ends, Dolly.

DOLLY: I hate to admit it but I can't deny it.

BEULAH: But they hang on together.

DOLLY: Yes, they hang on together.

BEULAH: Year after year after year, accumulating property and money, building up wealth and respect and position in the towns they live in and the counties and cities and the churches they go to, belonging to the clubs and so on and so forth and not a soul but them knowin' they have to go wash their hands after touching something the other one just put down! ha ha ha ha ha!—

DOLLY: Beulah, that's an evil laugh of yours, that laugh of yours is evil!

BEULAH [louder]: Ha ha ha ha ha! —But you know it's the truth.

DOLLY: Yes, she's tellin' the truth! [Nods to audience.]

BEULAH: Then one of them—gits—cincer or has a—stroke or somethin'? —The other one—

DOLLY: —Hauls in the loot?

BEULAH: That's right, hauls in the loot! Oh, my, then you should see how him or her blossoms out. New house, new car, new clothes. Some of 'em even change to a different church! —If it's a widow, she goes with a younger man, and if it's a widower, he starts courtin' some chick, ha ha ha ha ha! And so I said, I said to Lady this morning before she left for Mamphis to bring Jabe home, I said, "Lady, I don't suppose you're going to reopen the confectionery till Jabe is completely recovered from his operation." She said, "It can't wait for anything that might take that much time." Those are her exact words. It can't wait for anything that might take that much time. Too much is invested in it. It's going to be done over, redecorated, and opened on schedule the Saturday before Easter this spring! —Why?—Because—she knows Jabe is dying and she wants to clean up quick!

DOLLY: An awful thought. But a true one. Most awful thoughts are.

[*They are startled by sudden light laughter from the dim up-stage area. The light changes on the stage to mark a division.*]

SCENE ONE

The women turn to see Carol Cutrere in the archway between the store and the confectionery. She is past thirty and, lacking prettiness, she has an odd, fugitive beauty which is stressed, almost to the point of fantasy, by a style of make-up with which a dancer named Valli has lately made such an impression in the bohemian centers of France and Italy, the face and lips powdered white and the eyes outlined and exaggerated with black pencil and the lids tinted blue. Her family name is the oldest and most distinguished in the county.

BEULAH: Somebody don't seem to know that the store is closed.

DOLLY: Beulah?

BEULAH: What?

DOLLY: Can you understand how anybody would deliberately make themselves look fantastic as that?

BEULAH: Some people have to show off, it's a passion with them, anything on earth to get attention.

DOLLY: I sure wouldn't care for that kind of attention. Not me. I wouldn't desire it. . . .

[*During these lines, just loud enough for her to hear them, Carol has crossed to the pay-phone and deposited a coin.*]

CAROL: I want Tulane 0370 in New Orleans. What? Oh. Hold on a minute.

[*Eva Temple is descending the stairs, slowly, as if awed by Carol's appearance, Carol rings open the cashbox and removes some coins; returns to deposit coins in phone.*]

BEULAH: She helped herself to money out of the cashbox.

[*Eva passes Carol like a timid child skirting a lion cage.*]

CAROL: Hello, Sister.

EVA: I'm Eva.

CAROL: Hello, Eva.

EVA: Hello . . . [*Then in a loud whisper to Beulah and Dolly.*] She took money out of the cashbox.

DOLLY: Oh, she can do as she pleases, she's a Cutrere!

BEULAH: Shoot . . .

EVA: What is she doin' barefooted?

BEULAH: The last time she was arrested on the highway, they say that she was naked under her coat.

CAROL [*to operator*]: I'm waiting. [*Then to women.*] —I caught the heel of my slipper in that rotten boardwalk out there and it broke right off. [*Raises slippers in hand.*] They say if you break the heel of your slipper in the morning it means you'll meet the love of your life before dark. But it was already dark when I broke the heel of my slipper. Maybe that means I'll meet the love of my life before daybreak. [*The quality of her voice is curiously clear and childlike. Sister Temple appears on stair landing bearing an old waffle iron.*]

SISTER: Wasn't that them?

EVA: No, it was Carol Cutrere!

CAROL [*at phone*]: Just keep on ringing, please, he's probably drunk. [*Sister crosses by her as Eva did.*] Sometimes it takes quite a while to get through the living-room furniture. . . .

SISTER: —She a *sight?*

EVA: Uh-huh!

CAROL: Bertie?—Carol! —Hi, doll! Did you trip over something? I heard a crash. Well, I'm leaving right now, I'm already on the highway and everything's fixed, I've got my allowance back on condition that I remain forever away from Two River County! I had to blackmail them a little. I came to dinner with my eyes made up and my little black sequin jacket and Betsy Boo, my brother's wife, said, "Carol, you going out to a fancy dress ball?" I said, "Oh, no, I'm just going jooking tonight up and down the Dixie Highway between here and Memphis like I used to when I lived here." Why, honey, she flew so fast you couldn't see her passing and came back in with the ink still wet on the check! And this will be done once a month as long as I stay away from Two River County. . . . [Laughs gaily.] —How's Jackie? Bless his heart, give him a sweet kiss for me! Oh, honey, I'm driving straight through, not even stopping for pickups unless you need one! I'll meet you in the Starlite Lounge before it closes, or if I'm irresistibly delayed, I'll certainly join you for coffee at the Morning Call before the all-night places have closed for the day . . . —I—Bertie? Bertie? [Laughs uncertainly and hangs up.] —let's see, now. . . . [Removes a revolver from her trench coat pocket and crosses to fill it with cartridges back of counter.]

EVA: What she looking for?

SISTER: Ask her.

EVA [advancing]: What're you looking for, Carol?

CAROL: Cartridges for my revolver.

DOLLY: She don't have a license to carry a pistol.

BEULAH: She don't have a license to drive a car.

CAROL: When I stop for someone I want to be sure it's someone I want to stop for.

DOLLY: Sheriff Talbott ought to know about this when he gits back from the depot.

CAROL: Tell him, ladies. I've already given him notice that if he ever attempts to stop me again on the highway, I'll shoot it out with him. . . .

BEULAH: When anybody has trouble with the law—

[*Her sentence is interrupted by a panicky scream from Eva, immediately repeated by Sister. The Temple Sisters scramble upstairs to the landing. Dolly also cries out and turns, covering her face. A Negro Conjure Man has entered the store. His tattered garments are fantastically bedizened with many talismans and good-luck charms of shell and bone and feather. His blue-black skin is daubed with cryptic signs in white paint.*]

DOLLY: Git him out, git him out, he's going to mark my baby!

BEULAH: Oh, shoot, Dolly. . . . [*Dolly has now fled after the Temple Sisters, to the landing of the stairs. The Conjure Man advances with a soft, rapid, toothless mumble of words that sound like wind in dry grass. He is holding out something in his shaking hand.*] It's just that old crazy conjure man from Blue Mountain. He cain't mark your baby.

[*Phrase of primitive music or percussion as Negro moves into light. Beulah follows Dolly to landing.*]

CAROL [*very high and clear voice*]: Come here, Uncle, and let me see what you've got there. Oh, it's a bone of some kind. No, I don't want to touch it, it isn't clean yet, there's still some flesh clinging to it. [*Women make sounds of revulsion.*] Yes, I know it's the breastbone of a bird but it's still tainted with corruption. Leave it a long time on a bare rock in the rain and the sun till every sign of corruption is burned and washed away from it, and then it

21

will be a good charm, a white charm, but now it's a black charm, Uncle. So take it away and do what I told you with it. . . .

[*The Negro makes a ducking obeisance and shuffles slowly back to the door.*]

Hey, Uncle Pleasant, give us the Choctaw cry.

[*Negro stops in confectionery.*]

He's part Choctaw, he knows the Choctaw cry.

SISTER TEMPLE: Don't let him holler in *here!*

CAROL: Come on, Uncle Pleasant, *you* know it!

[*She takes off her coat, sits on right window sill. She starts the cry herself. The Negro throws back his head and completes it: a series of barking sounds that rise to a high, sustained note of wild intensity. The women on the landing retreat further upstairs. Just then, as though the cry had brought him, Val enters the store. He is a young man, about thirty, who has a kind of wild beauty about him that the cry would suggest. He does not wear Levi's or a T-shirt, he has on a pair of dark serge pants, glazed from long wear and not excessively tight-fitting. His remarkable garment is a snakeskin jacket, mottled white, black and gray. He carries a guitar which is covered with inscriptions.*]

CAROL [*looking at the young man*]: Thanks, Uncle . . .

BEULAH: *Hey, old man, you! Choctaw! Conjure man! Nigguh! Will you go out-a this sto'? So we can come back downstairs?*

[*Carol hands the Negro a dollar; he goes out cackling. Val holds the door open for Vee Talbott, a heavy, vague woman in her forties. She does primitive oil paintings and carries one into the store, saying:*]

VEE: I got m'skirt caught in th' door of the Chevrolet an' I'm afraid I tore it. [*The women descend into store: laconic greetings, interest focused on Val.*] Is it dark in here or am I losin' my eyesight? I been painting all day, finished a picture in a ten-hour stretch, just stopped a few minutes fo' coffee and went back to it again while I had a clear vision. I think I got it this time. But I'm so exhausted I could drop in my tracks. There's nothing more exhausting than that kind of work on earth, it's not so much that it tires your body out, but it leaves you drained inside. Y'know what I mean? Inside? Like you was burned out by something? Well! Still! —You feel you've accomplished something when you're through with it, sometimes you feel—*elevated!* How are you, Dolly?

DOLLY: All right, Mrs. Talbott.

VEE: That's good. How are *you*, Beulah?

BEULAH: Oh, I'm all right, I reckon.

VEE: Still can't make out much. Who is that there? [*Indicates Carol's figure by the window. A significant silence greets this question. Then, suddenly:*] *Oh!* I thought her folks had got her out of the county . . .

[*Carol utters a very light, slightly rueful laugh, her eyes drifting back to Val as she moves back into confectionery.*]

Jabe and Lady back yet?

DOLLY: Pee Wee an' Dawg have gone to the depot to meet 'em.

VEE: Aw. Well, I'm just in time. I brought my new picture with me, the paint isn't dry on it yet. I thought that Lady might want to hang it up in Jabe's room while he's convalescin' from the operation, cause after a close shave with death, people like to be reminded of spiritual things. Huh? Yes! This is the Holy Ghost ascending. . . .

DOLLY [*looking at canvas*]: You didn't put a head on it.

VEE: The head was a blaze of light, that's all I saw in my vision.

DOLLY: Who's the young man with yuh?

VEE: Aw, excuse me, I'm too worn out to have manners. This is Mr. Valentine Xavier, Mrs. Hamma and Mrs. —I'm sorry, Beulah. I never *can* get y' last *name!*

BEULAH: I fo'give you. My name is Beulah Binnings.

VAL: What shall I do with this here?

VEE: Oh, that bowl of sherbet. I thought that Jabe might need something light an' digestible so I brought a bowl of sherbet.

DOLLY: What flavor is it?

VEE: Pineapple.

DOLLY: Oh, goody, I love pineapple. Better put it in the icebox before it starts to melt.

BEULAH [*looking under napkin that covers bowl*]: I'm afraid you're lockin' th' stable after the horse is gone.

DOLLY: Aw, is it melted already?

BEULAH: Reduced to juice.

VEE: Aw, shoot. Well, put it on ice anyhow, it might thicken up. [*Women are still watching Val.*] Where's the icebox?

BEULAH: In the confectionery.

VEE: I thought that Lady had closed the confectionery.

BEULAH: Yes, but the Frigidaire's still there.

[*Val goes out right through confectionery.*]

VEE: Mr. Xavier is a stranger in our midst. His car broke down in that storm last night and I let him sleep in the lockup. He's lookin' for work and I thought I'd introduce him to Lady an' Jabe because if Jabe can't work they're going to need somebody to help out in th' store.

BEULAH: That's a good idea.

DOLLY: Uh-huh.

BEULAH: Well, come on in, you all, it don't look like they're comin' straight home from the depot anyhow.

DOLLY: Maybe that wasn't the Cannonball Express.

BEULAH: Or maybe they stopped off fo' Pee Wee to buy some liquor.

DOLLY: Yeah . . . at Ruby Lightfoot's.

[*They move past Carol and out of sight. Carol has risen. Now she crosses into the main store area, watching Val with the candid curiosity of one child observing another. He pays no attention but concentrates on his belt buckle, which he is repairing with a pocketknife.*]

CAROL: What're you fixing?

VAL: Belt buckle.

CAROL: Boys like you are always fixing something. Could you fix my slipper?

VAL: What's wrong with your slipper?

CAROL: Why are you pretending not to remember me?

VAL: It's hard to remember someone you never met.

CAROL: Then why'd you look so startled when you saw me?

25

VAL: Did I?

CAROL: I thought for a moment you'd run back out the door.

VAL: The sight of a woman can make me walk in a hurry but I don't think it's ever made me run. —You're standing in my light.

CAROL [*moving aside slightly*]: Oh, excuse me. Better?

VAL: Thanks. . . .

CAROL: Are you afraid I'll snitch?

VAL: Do what?

CAROL: Snitch? I wouldn't; I'm not a snitch. But I can prove that I know you if I have to. It was New Year's Eve in New Orleans.

VAL: I need a small pair of pliers. . . .

CAROL: You had on that jacket and a snake ring with a ruby eye.

VAL: I never had a snake ring with a ruby eye.

CAROL: A snake ring with an emerald eye?

VAL: I never had a snake ring with any kind of an eye. . . . [*Begins to whistle softly, his face averted.*]

CAROL [*smiling gently*]: Then maybe it was a dragon ring with an emerald eye or a diamond or a ruby eye. You told us that it was a gift from a lady osteopath that you'd met somewhere in your travels and that any time you were broke you'd wire this lady osteopath collect, and no matter how far you were or how long it was since you'd seen her, she'd send you a money order for twenty-five dollars with the same sweet message each time. "I love you. When will you come back?" And to prove the story, not that it was difficult to believe it, you took the latest of these sweet messages from your wallet for us to see. . . . [*She throws back her head with soft laughter. He looks away still further and busies himself with the belt buckle.*] —We followed you through five places before we made contact with you and I was the one that made contact. I went up to the bar where you were standing and touched your jacket and said, "What stuff is this made of?" and when you said it was snakeskin, I said, "I wish you'd told me before I touched it." And you said something not nice. You said, "Maybe that will learn you to hold back your hands." I was drunk by that time, which was after midnight. Do you remember what I said to you? I said, "What on earth can you do on this earth but catch at whatever comes near you, with both your hands, until your fingers are broken?" I'd never said that before, or even consciously thought it, but afterwards it seemed like the truest thing that my lips had ever spoken, what on earth can you do but catch at whatever comes near you with both your hands until your fingers are broken. . . . You gave me a quick, sober look. I think you nodded slightly, and then you picked up your guitar and began to sing. After singing you passed the kitty. Whenever paper money was dropped in the kitty you blew a whistle. My cousin Bertie and I dropped in five dollars, you blew the whistle five times and then sat down at our table for a drink, Schenley's with Seven Up. You showed us all those signatures on your guitar. . . . Any correction so far?

VAL: Why are you so anxious to prove I know you?

CAROL: Because I want to know you better and better! I'd like to go out jooking with you tonight.

VAL: What's jooking?

CAROL: Oh, don't you know what that is? That's where you get in a car and drink a little and drive a little and stop and dance a little to a juke box and then you drink a little more and drive a little more and stop and dance a little more to a juke box and then you stop dancing and you just drink and drive and then you stop driving and just drink, and then, finally, you stop drinking. . . .

VAL: —What do you do, then?

CAROL: That depends on the weather and who you're jooking with. If it's a clear night you spread a blanket among the memorial stones on Cypress Hill, which is the local bone orchard, but if it's not a fair night, and this one certainly isn't, why, usually then you go to the Idlewild cabins between here and Sunset on the Dixie Highway. . . .

VAL: —That's about what I figured. But I don't go that route. Heavy drinking and smoking the weed and shacking with strangers is okay for kids in their twenties but this is my thirtieth birthday and I'm all through with that route. [*Looks up with dark eyes.*] I'm not young any more.

CAROL: You're young at thirty—I hope so! I'm twenty-nine!

VAL: Naw, you're not young at thirty if you've been on a goddam party since you were fifteen!

[*Picks up his guitar and sings and plays "Heavenly Grass." Carol has taken a pint of bourbon from her trench coat pocket and she passes it to him.*]

CAROL: Thanks. That's lovely. Many happy returns of your birthday, Snakeskin. [*She is very close to him. Vee enters and says sharply:*]

VEE: Mr. Xavier don't drink.

CAROL: Oh, ex-cuse *me!*

VEE: And if you behaved yourself better your father would not be paralyzed in bed!

[*Sound of car out front. Women come running with various cries. Lady enters, nodding to the women, and holding the door open for her husband and the men following him. She greets the women in almost toneless murmurs, as if too tired to speak. She could be any age between thirty-five and forty-five, in appearance, but her figure is youthful. Her face taut. She is a woman who met with emotional disaster in her girlhood; verges on hysteria under strain. Her voice is often shrill and her body tense. But when in repose, a girlish softness emerges again and she looks ten years younger.*]

LADY: Come in, Jabe. We've got a reception committee here to meet us. They've set up a buffet supper.

[*Jabe enters. A gaunt, wolfish man, gray and yellow. The women chatter idiotically.*]

BEULAH: Well, look who's here!

DOLLY: Well, *Jabe!*

BEULAH: I don't think he's been sick. I think he's been to Miami. Look at that wonderful color in his face!

DOLLY: I never seen him look better in my life!

BEULAH: Who does he think he's foolin'? Ha ha ha!— not *me!*

JABE: Whew, Jesus—I'm mighty—tired. . . .

[*An uncomfortable silence, everyone staring greedily at the dying man with his tense, wolfish smile and nervous cough.*]

PEE WEE: Well, Jabe, we been feedin' lots of nickels to those one-arm bandits in there.

DOG: An' that pinball machine is hotter'n a pistol.

PEE WEE: Ha ha.

[*Eva Temple appears on stairs and screams for her sister.*]

EVA: Sistuh! Sistuh! Sistuh! Cousin Jabe's here!

[*A loud clatter upstairs and shrieks.*]

JABE: Jesus. . . .

[*Eva rushing at him—stops short and bursts into tears.*]

LADY: Oh, cut that out, Eva Temple! —What were you doin' upstairs?

EVA: I can't help it, it's so good to see him, it's so wonderful to see our cousin again, oh, Jabe, *blessed!*

SISTER: Where's Jabe, where's precious Jabe? Where's our precious cousin?

EVA: Right here, Sister!

SISTER: Well, bless your old sweet life, and lookit the color he's got in his face, will you?

BEULAH: I just told him he looks like he's been to Miami and got a Florida suntan, ha ha ha!

[*The preceding speeches are very rapid, all overlapping.*]

JABE: I ain't been out in no sun an' if you all will excuse me I'm gonna do my celebratin' upstairs in bed because I'm kind of— worn out. [*Goes creakily to foot of steps while Eva and Sister sob into their handkerchiefs behind him.*] —I see they's been some changes made here. Uh-huh. Uh-huh. How come the shoe department's back here now? [*Instant hostility as if habitual between them.*]

LADY: We always had a problem with light in this store.

JABE: So you put the shoe department further away from the

window? That's sensible. A very intelligent solution to the problem, Lady.

LADY: Jabe, you know I told you we got a fluorescent tube coming to put back here.

JABE: Uh-huh. Uh-huh. Well. Tomorrow I'll get me some niggers to help me move the shoe department back front.

LADY: You do whatever you want to, it's your store.

JABE: Uh-huh. Uh-huh. I'm glad you reminded me of it.

[*Lady turns sharply away. He starts up stairs. Pee Wee and Dog follow him up. The women huddle and whisper in the store. Lady sinks wearily into chair at table.*]

BEULAH: That man will never come down those stairs again!

DOLLY: Never in this world, honey.

BEULAH: He has th' death sweat on him! Did you notice that death sweat on him?

DOLLY: An' yellow as butter, just as yellow as—

[*Sister sobs.*]

EVA: Sister, Sister!

BEULAH [*crossing to Lady*]: Lady, I don't suppose you feel much like talking about it right now but Dog and me are so worried.

DOLLY: Pee Wee and me are worried sick about it.

LADY: —About what?

BEULAH: Jabe's operation in Memphis. Was it successful?

DOLLY: Wasn't it successful?

[*Lady stares at them blindly. The women, except Carol, close avidly about her, tense with morbid interest.*]

SISTER: Was it too late for surgical interference?

EVA: Wasn't it successful?

[*A loud, measured knock begins on the floor above.*]

BEULAH: Somebody told us it had gone past the knife.

DOLLY: We do hope it ain't hopeless.

EVA: We hope and pray it ain't hopeless.

[*All their faces wear faint, unconscious smiles. Lady looks from face to face; then utters a slight, startled laugh and springs up from the table and crosses to the stairs.*]

LADY [*as if in flight*]: Excuse me, I have to go up, Jabe's knocking for me. [*Lady goes upstairs. The women gaze after her.*]

CAROL [*suddenly and clearly, in the silence*]: Speaking of knocks, I have a knock in my engine. It goes knock, knock, and I say who's there. I don't know whether I'm in communication with some dead ancestor or the motor's about to drop out and leave me stranded in the dead of night on the Dixie Highway. Do you have any knowledge of mechanics? I'm sure you do. Would you be sweet and take a short drive with me? So you could hear that knock?

VAL: I don't have time.

CAROL: What have you got to do?

VAL: I'm waiting to see about a job in this store.

CAROL: I'm offering you a job.

VAL: I want a job that pays.

CAROL: I expect to pay you.

[*Women whisper loudly in the background.*]

VAL: Maybe sometime tomorrow.

CAROL: I can't stay here overnight; I'm not allowed to stay overnight in this county.

[*Whispers rise. The word "corrupt" is distinguished. Then Carol, without turning, smiles very brightly.*]

What are they saying about me? Can you hear what those women are saying about me?

VAL: —Play it cool. . . .

CAROL: I don't like playing it cool! What are they saying about me? That I'm corrupt?

VAL: If you don't want to be talked about, why do you make up like that, why do you—

CAROL: *To show off!*

VAL: What?

CAROL: *I'm an exhibitionist!* I want to be noticed, seen, heard, felt! I want them to know I'm alive! Don't you want them to know you're alive?

VAL: I want to live and I don't care if they know I'm alive or not.

CAROL: Then why do you play a guitar?

VAL: Why do you make a goddam show of yourself?

CAROL: That's right, for the same reason.

VAL: We don't go the same route. . . . [*He keeps moving away from her; she continually follows him. Her speech is compulsive.*]

CAROL: I used to be what they call a Christ-bitten reformer. You know what that is? —A kind of benign exhibitionist. . . . I delivered stump speeches, wrote letters of protest about the gradual massacre of the colored majority in the county. I thought it was wrong for pellagra and slow starvation to cut them down when the cotton crop failed from army worm or boll weevil or too much rain in summer. I wanted to, tried to, put up free clinics, I squandered the money my mother left me on it. And when that Willie McGee thing came along—he was sent to the chair for having improper relations with a white whore— [*Her voice is like a passionate incantation.*] I made a fuss about it. I put on a potato sack and set out for the capital on foot. This was in winter. I walked barefoot in this burlap sack to deliver a personal protest to the governor of the state. Oh, I suppose it was partly exhibitionism on my part, but it wasn't completely exhibitionism; there was something else in it, too. You know how far I got? Six miles out of town—hooted, jeered at, even spit on!—every step of the way—and then arrested! Guess what for? Lewd vagrancy! Uh-huh, that was the charge, "lewd vagrancy," because they said that potato sack I had on was not a respectable garment. . . . Well, all that was a pretty long time ago, and now I'm not a reformer any more. I'm just a "lewd vagrant." And I'm showing the "S.O.B.S." how lewd a "lewd vagrant" can be if she puts her whole heart in it like I do mine! All right. I've told you my story, the story of an exhibitionist. Now I want you to do something for me. Take me out to Cypress Hill in my car. And we'll hear the dead people talk. They do talk there. They chatter together like birds on Cypress Hill, but all they say is one word and that one word is "live," they say, "Live, live, live, live, live!" It's all they've learned, it's the only advice they can give. —Just live. . . . [*She opens the door.*] Simple!—a very simple instruction. . . .

[*Goes out. Women's voices rise from the steady, indistinct murmur, like hissing geese.*]

WOMEN'S VOICES: —No, not liquor! Dope!

—Something not normal all right!

—Her father and brother were warned by the Vigilantes to keep her out of this county.

—She's absolutely degraded!

—Yes, corrupt!

—Corrupt! (*Etc., etc.*)

[*As if repelled by their hissing voices, Val suddenly picks up his guitar and goes out of the store as—Vee Talbott appears on the landing and calls down to him.*]

VEE: Mr. Xavier! Where is Mr. Xavier?

BEULAH: Gone, honey.

DOLLY: You might as well face it, Vee. This is one candidate for salvation that you have lost to the opposition.

BEULAH: He's gone off to Cypress Hill with the Cutrere girl.

VEE [*descending*]: —If some of you older women in Two River County would set a better example there'd be more decent young people!

BEULAH: What was that remark?

VEE: I mean that people who give drinkin' parties an' get so drunk they don't know which is their husband and which is somebody else's and people who serve on the altar guild and still play cards on Sundays—

BEULAH: Just stop right there! Now I've discovered the source of that dirty gossip!

VEE: I'm only repeating what I've been told by others. I never been to these parties!

BEULAH: No, and you never will! You're a public killjoy, a professional hypocrite!

VEE: I try to build up characters! You and your drinkin' parties are only concerned with tearin' characters down! I'm goin' upstairs, I'm goin' back upstairs! [*Rushes upstairs.*]

BEULAH: Well, I'm glad I said what I said to that woman. I've got no earthly patience with that sort of hypocriticism. Dolly, let's put this perishable stuff in the Frigidaire and leave here. I've never been so thoroughly disgusted!

DOLLY: Oh, my Lawd. [*Pauses at stairs and shouts:*] PEE WEE! [*Goes off with the dishes.*]

SISTER: Both of those wimmen are as common as dirt.

EVA: Dolly's folks in Blue Mountain are nothin' at all but the poorest kind of white trash. Why, Lollie Tucker told me the old man sits on the porch with his shoes off drinkin' beer out of a bucket! —Let's take these flowers with us to put on the altar.

SISTER: Yes, we can give Jabe credit in the parish notes.

EVA: I'm going to take these olive-nut sandwiches, too. They'll come in handy for the Bishop Adjutant's tea.

[*Dolly and Beulah cross through.*]

DOLLY: We still have time to make the second show.

BEULAH [*shouting*]: Dog!

DOLLY: Pee Wee! [*They rush out of store.*]

EVA: Sits on the porch with his shoes off?

SISTER: Drinkin' beer out of a bucket! [*They go out with umbrellas, etc. Men descend stairs.*]

TALBOTT: Well, it looks to me like Jabe will more than likely go under before the cotton comes up.

PEE WEE: He never looked good.

DOG: Naw, but now he looks worse. [*They cross to door.*]

TALBOTT: Vee!

VEE [*from landing*]: Hush that bawling. I had to speak to Lady about that boy and I couldn't speak to her in front of Jabe because he thinks he's gonna be able to go back to work himself.

TALBOTT: Well, move along, quit foolin'.

VEE: I think I ought to wait till that boy gits back.

TALBOTT: I'm sick of you making a goddam fool of yourself over every stray bastard that wanders into this county.

[*Car horn honks loudly, Vee follows her husband out. Sound of cars driving off. Dogs bay in distance as lights dim to indicate short passage of time.*]

SCENE TWO

A couple of hours later that night. Through the great window the landscape is faintly luminous under a scudding moonlit sky. Outside a girl's laughter, Carol's, rings out high and clear and is followed by the sound of a motor, rapidly going off.

Val enters the store before the car sound quite fades out and while a dog is still barking at it somewhere along the highway. He says "Christ" under his breath, goes to the buffet table and scrubs lipstick stain off his mouth and face with a paper napkin, picks up his guitar, which he had left on a counter.

Footsteps descending: Lady appears on the landing in a flannel robe, shivering in the cold air; she snaps her fingers impatiently for the old dog, Bella, who comes limping down beside her. She doesn't see Val, seated on the shadowy counter, and she goes directly to the phone near the stairs. Her manner is desperate, her voice harsh and shrill.

LADY: Ge' me the drugstore, will you? I know the drugstore's closed, this is Mrs. Torrance, my store's closed, too, but I got a sick man here, just back from the hospital, yeah, yeah, an emergency, wake up Mr. Dubinsky, keep ringing till he answers, it's an emergency! [*Pause: she mutters under her breath:*] —Porca la miseria! —I wish I was dead, dead, dead. . . .

VAL [*quietly*]: No, you don't, lady.

[*She gasps, turning and seeing him, without leaving the phone, she rings the cashbox open and snatches out something.*]

LADY: What're you doin' here? You know this store is closed!

VAL: I seen a light was still on and the door was open so I come back to—

LADY: You see what I got in my hand? [*Raises revolver above level of counter.*]

VAL: You going to shoot me?

LADY: You better believe it if you don't get out of here, mister!

VAL: That's all right, Lady, I just come back to pick up my guitar.

LADY: To pick up your guitar?

[*He lifts it gravely.*]

—Huh. . . .

VAL: Mizz Talbott brought me here. I was here when you got back from Memphis, don't you remember?

LADY: —Aw. Aw, yeah. . . . You been here all this time?

VAL: No. I went out and come back.

LADY [*into the phone*]: I told you to keep ringing till he answers! Go on, keep ringing, keep ringing! [*Then to Val:*] You went out and come back?

VAL: Yeah.

LADY: What for?

VAL: You know that girl that was here?

LADY: Carol Cutrere?

VAL: She said she had car trouble and could I fix it.

LADY: —Did you fix it?

VAL: She didn't have no car trouble, that wasn't her trouble, oh, she had trouble, all right, but *that* wasn't it. . . .

LADY: What was her trouble?

VAL: She made a mistake about me.

LADY: What mistake?

VAL: She thought I had a sign "Male at Stud" hung on me.

LADY: She thought you—? [*Into phone suddenly:*] Oh, Mr. Dubinsky, I'm sorry to wake you up but I just brought my husband back from the Memphis hospital and I left my box of Luminal tablets in the—I got to have some! I ain't slep' for three nights, I'm going to pieces, you hear me, I'm going to pieces, I ain't slept in three nights, I got to have some tonight. Now you look here, if you want to keep my trade, you send me over some tablets. Then bring them yourself, God damn it, excuse my French! Because I'm going to pieces right this minute! [*Hangs up violently.*] —*Mannage la miseria!* —Christ. . . . I'm shivering! —It's cold as a goddam ice plant in this store, I don't know why, it never seems to hold heat, the ceiling's too high or something, it don't hold heat at all. —Now what do you want? I got to go upstairs.

VAL: Here. Put this on you. [*He removes his jacket and hands it to her. She doesn't take it at once, stares at him questioningly and then slowly takes the jacket in her hands and examines it, running her fingers curiously over the snakeskin.*]

LADY: What is this stuff this thing's made of? It looks like it was snakeskin.

VAL: Yeah, well, that's what it is.

LADY: What're you doing with a snakeskin jacket?

VAL: It's a sort of a trademark; people call me Snakeskin.

LADY: Who calls you Snakeskin?

VAL: Oh, in the bars, the sort of places I work in—but I've quit that. I'm through with that stuff now. . . .

LADY: You're a—entertainer?

VAL: I sing and play the guitar.

LADY: —Aw? [*She puts the jacket on as if to explore it.*] It feels warm all right.

VAL: It's warm from my body, I guess. . . .

LADY: You must be a warm-blooded boy. . . .

VAL: That's right. . . .

LADY: Well, what in God's name are you lookin' for around here?

VAL: —Work.

LADY: Boys like you don't work.

VAL: What d'you mean by boys like me?

LADY: Ones that play th' guitar and go around talkin' about how warm they are. . . .

VAL: That happens t' be the truth. My temperature's always a couple degrees above normal the same as a dog's, it's normal for me the same as it is for a dog, that's the truth. . . .

LADY: —Huh!

VAL: You don't believe me?

LADY: I have no reason to doubt you, but what about it?

VAL: —Why—nothing. . . .

[*Lady laughs softly and suddenly; Val smiles slowly and warmly.*]

LADY: You're a peculiar somebody all right, you sure are! How did you get around here?

VAL: I was driving through here last night and an axle broke on my car, that stopped me here, and I went to the county jail for a place to sleep out of the rain. Mizz Talbott took me in and give me a cot in the lockup and said if I hung around till you got back that you might give me a job in the store to help out since your husband was tooken sick.

LADY: —Uh-huh. Well—she was wrong about that. . . . If I took on help here it would have to be local help, I couldn't hire no stranger with a—snakeskin jacket and a guitar . . . and that runs a temperature as high as a dog's! [*Throws back her head in another soft, sudden laugh and starts to take off the jacket.*]

VAL: Keep it on.

LADY: No, I got to go up now and you had better be going . . .

VAL: I got nowhere to go.

LADY: Well, everyone's got a problem and that's yours.

VAL: —What nationality are you?

LADY: Why do you ask me that?

VAL: You seem to be like a foreigner.

LADY: I'm the daughter of a Wop bootlegger burned to death in his orchard! —Take your jacket. . . .

VAL: What was that you said about your father?

LADY: Why?

VAL: —A "Wop bootlegger"?

LADY: —They burned him to death in his orchard! What about it? The story's well known around here. [*Jabe knocks on ceiling.*] I got to go up, I'm being called for.

[*She turns out light over counter and at the same moment he begins to sing softly with his guitar: "Heavenly Grass." He suddenly stops short and says abruptly:*]

VAL: I do electric repairs. [*Lady stares at him softly.*] I can do all kinds of odd jobs. Lady, I'm thirty today and I'm through with the life that I've been leading. [*Pause. Dog bays in distance.*] I lived in corruption but I'm not corrupted. Here is why. [*Picks up his guitar.*] My life's companion! It washes me clean like water when anything unclean has touched me. . . . [*Plays softly, with a slow smile.*]

LADY: What's all that writing on it?

VAL: Autographs of musicians I run into here and there.

LADY: Can I see it?

VAL: Turn on that light above you.

[*She switches on green-shaded bulb over counter. Val holds the instrument tenderly between them as if it were a child; his voice is soft, intimate, tender.*]

See this name? Leadbelly?

LADY: Leadbelly?

VAL: Greatest man ever lived on the twelve-string guitar! Played it so good he broke the stone heart of a Texas governor with it and won himself a pardon out of jail. . . . And see this name Oliver? King Oliver? That name is immortal, Lady. Greatest man since Gabriel on a horn. . . .

LADY: What's this name?

VAL: Oh. That name? That name is also immortal. The name Bessie Smith is written in the stars! —Jim Crow killed her, John

Barleycorn and Jim Crow killed Bessie Smith but that's another story. . . . See this name here? That's another immortal!

LADY: Fats Waller? Is his name written in the stars, too?

VAL: Yes, his name is written in the stars, too. . . .

[*Her voice is also intimate and soft: a spell of softness between them, their bodies almost touching, only divided by the guitar.*]

LADY: You had any sales experience?

VAL: All my life I been selling something to someone.

LADY: So's everybody. You got any character reference on you?

VAL: I have this—letter. [*Removes a worn, folded letter from a wallet, dropping a lot of snapshots and cards of various kinds on the floor. He passes the letter to her gravely and crouches to collect the dropped articles while she peruses the character reference.*]

LADY [*reading slowly aloud*]: "This boy worked for me three months in my auto repair shop and is a real hard worker and is good and honest but is a peculiar talker and that is the reason I got to let him go but would like to— [*Holds letter closer to light.*] — would like to—keep him. Yours truly." [*Val stares at her gravely, blinking a little.*] Huh! —Some reference!

VAL: —Is that what it says?

LADY: Didn't you know what it said?

VAL: No. —The man sealed the envelope on it.

LADY: Well, that's not the sort of character reference that will do you much good, boy.

VAL: Naw. I guess it ain't.

LADY: —However. . . .

VAL: —What?

LADY: What people say about you don't mean much. Can you read shoe sizes?

VAL: I guess so.

LADY: What does 75 David mean? [*Val stares at her, shakes head slowly.*] 75 means seven and one half long and David mean "D" wide. You know how to make change?

VAL: Yeah, I could make change in a store.

LADY: Change for better or worse? Ha ha! —Well— [*Pause.*] Well—you see that other room there, through that arch there? That's the confectionery; it's closed now but it's going to be re-opened in a short while and I'm going to compete for the night life in this county, the after-the-movies trade. I'm going to serve setups in there and I'm going to redecorate. I got it all planned. [*She is talking eagerly now, as if to herself.*] Artificial branches of fruit trees in flower on the walls and ceilings! —It's going to be like an orchard in the spring! —My father, he had an orchard on Moon Lake. He made a wine garden of it. We had fifteen little white arbors with tables in them and they were covered with—grapevines and—we sold Dago red wine an' bootleg whiskey and beer. —They burned it up! My father was burned up in it. . . .

[*Jabe knocks above more loudly and a hoarse voice shouts "Lady!" Figure appears at the door and calls: "Mrs. Torrance?"*]

Oh, that's the sandman with my sleeping tablets. [*Crosses to door.*] Thanks, Mr. Dubinsky, sorry I had to disturb you, sorry I— [*Man mutters something and goes. She closes the door.*] Well, go to hell, then, old bastard. . . . [*Returns with package.*] —You ever have trouble sleeping?

VAL: I can sleep or not sleep as long or short as I want to.

LADY: Is that right?

VAL: I can sleep on a concrete floor or go without sleeping, without even feeling sleepy, for forty-eight hours. And I can hold my breath three minutes without blacking out; I made ten dollars betting I could do it and I did it! And I can go a whole day without passing water.

LADY [*startled*]: Is *that* a *fact?*

VAL [*very simply as if he'd made an ordinary remark*]: That's a fact. I served time on a chain gang for vagrancy once and they tied me to a post all day and I stood there all day without passing water to show the sons of bitches that I could do it.

LADY: —I see what that auto repair man was talking about when he said this boy is a peculiar talker! Well—what else can you do? Tell me some more about your self-control!

VAL [*grinning*]: Well, they say that a woman can burn a man down. But I can burn down a woman.

LADY: Which woman?

VAL: Any two-footed woman.

LADY [*throws back her head in sudden friendly laughter as he grins at her with the simple candor of a child*]: —Well, there's lots of two-footed women round here that might be willin' to test the truth of that statement.

VAL: I'm saying I could. I'm not saying I would.

LADY: Don't worry, boy. I'm one two-footed woman that you don't have to convince of your perfect controls.

VAL: No, I'm done with all that.

LADY: What's the matter? Have they tired you out?

VAL: I'm not tired. I'm disgusted.

LADY: Aw, you're disgusted, huh?

VAL: I'm telling you, Lady, there's people bought and sold in this world like carcasses of hogs in butcher shops!

LADY: You ain't tellin' me nothin' I don't know.

VAL: You might think there's many and many kinds of people in this world but, Lady, there's just two kinds of people, the ones that are bought and the buyers! No!—there's one other kind . . .

LADY: What kind's that?

VAL: The kind that's never been branded.

LADY: You will be, man.

VAL: They got to catch me first.

LADY: Well, then, you better not settle down in this county.

VAL: You know they's a kind of bird that don't have legs so it can't light on nothing but has to stay all its life on its wings in the sky? That's true. I seen one once, it had died and fallen to earth and it was light-blue colored and its body was tiny as your little finger, that's the truth, it had a body as tiny as your little finger and so light on the palm of your hand it didn't weigh more than a feather, but its wings spread out this wide but they was transparent, the color of the sky and you could see through them. That's what they call protection coloring. Camouflage, they call it. You can't tell those birds from the sky and that's why the hawks don't catch them, don't see them up there in the high blue sky near the sun!

LADY: How about in gray weather?

VAL: They fly so high in gray weather the goddam hawks would get dizzy. But those little birds, they don't have no legs at all and

47

they live their whole lives on the wing, and they sleep on the wind, that's how they sleep at night, they just spread their wings and go to sleep on the wind like other birds fold their wings and go to sleep on a tree. . . . [*Music fades in.*] —They sleep on the wind and . . . [*His eyes grow soft and vague and he lifts his guitar and accompanies the very faint music.*] —never light on this earth but one time when they die!

LADY: —I'd like to be one of those birds.

VAL: So'd I like to be one of those birds; they's lots of people would like to be one of those birds and never be—corrupted!

LADY: If one of those birds ever dies and falls on the ground and you happen to find it, I wish you would show it to me because I think maybe you just imagine there is a bird of that kind in existence. Because I don't think nothing living has ever been that free, not even nearly. Show me one of them birds and I'll say, Yes, God's made one perfect creature! —I sure would give this mercantile store and every bit of stock in it to be that tiny bird the color of the sky . . . for one night to sleep on the wind and—float!— around under th'—stars . . . [*Jabe knocks on floor, Lady's eyes return to Val.*] —Because I sleep with a son of a bitch who bought me at a fire sale, and not in fifteen years have I had a single good dream, not one—oh! —*Shit* . . . I don't know why I'm—telling a stranger—this. . . . [*She rings the cashbox open.*] Take this dollar and go eat at the Al-Nite on the highway and come back here in the morning and I'll put you to work. I'll break you in clerking here and when the new confectionery opens, well, maybe I can use you in there. —That door locks when you close it! —But let's get one thing straight.

VAL: What thing?

LADY: I'm not interested in your perfect functions, in fact you don't interest me no more than the air that you stand in. If that's understood we'll have a good working relation, but otherwise trouble! —Of course I know you're crazy, but they's lots of crazier people than you are still running loose and some of them in high positions, too. Just remember. No monkey business with me. Now go. Go eat, you're hungry.

VAL: Mind if I leave this here? My life's companion? [*He means his guitar.*]

LADY: Leave it here if you want to.

VAL: Thanks, Lady.

LADY: Don't mention it.

[*He crosses toward the door as a dog barks with passionate clarity in the distance. He turns to smile back at her and says:*]

VAL: I don't know nothing about you except you're nice but you are just about the nicest person that I have ever run into! And I'm going to be steady and honest and hardworking to please you and any time you have any more trouble sleeping, I know how to fix that for you. A lady osteopath taught me how to make little adjustments in the neck and spine that give you sound, natural sleep. Well, g'night, now.

[*He goes out. Count five. Then she throws back her head and laughs as lightly and gaily as a young girl. Then she turns and wonderingly picks up and runs her hands tenderly over his guitar as the curtain falls.*]

The store, afternoon, a few weeks later. The table and chair are back in the confectionery. Lady is hanging up the phone. Val is standing just outside the door. He turns and enters. Outside on the highway a mule team is laboring to pull a big truck back on the icy pavement. A Negro's voice shouts: "Hyyyyyyyyyyy-up."

VAL [*moving to right window*]: One a them big Diamond T trucks an' trailors gone off the highway last night and a six-mule team is tryin' t' pull it back on. . . . [*He looks out window.*]

LADY [*coming from behind to right of counter*]: Mister, we just now gotten a big fat complaint about you from a woman that says if she wasn't a widow her husband would come in here and beat the tar out of you.

VAL [*taking a step toward her*]: Yeah?—Is this a small pink-headed woman?

LADY: *Pin*-headed woman did you say?

VAL: Naw, I said, "Pink!"—A little pink-haired woman, in a checkered coat with pearl buttons this big on it.

LADY: I talked to her on the phone. She didn't go into such details about her appearance but she did say you got familiar. I said, "How? by his talk or behavior?" And she said, "Both!"—Now I was afraid of this when I warned you last week, "No monkey business here, boy!"

VAL: This little pink-headed woman bought a valentine from me and all I said is my *name* is Valentine to her. Few minutes later a small colored boy come in and delivered the valentine to me with something wrote on it an' I believe I still got it. . . . [*Finds and shows it to Lady who goes to him. Lady reads it, and tears it fiercely to pieces. He lights a cigarette.*]

LADY: Signed it with a lipstick kiss? You didn't show up for this date?

VAL: No, ma'am. That's why she complained. [*Throws match on floor.*]

LADY: Pick that match up off the floor.

VAL: Are you bucking for sergeant, or something? [*He throws match out the door with elaborate care. Her eyes follow his back. Val returns lazily toward her.*]

LADY: Did you walk around in front of her that way?

VAL [*at counter*]: What way?

LADY: Slew-foot, slew-foot!

[*He regards her closely with good-humored perplexity.*]

Did you stand in front of her like that? That close? In that, that—*position?*

VAL: What position?

LADY: Ev'rything you do is suggestive!

VAL: Suggestive of what?

LADY: Of what you said you was through with—somethin'— *Oh, shoot, you know what I mean.* —Why'd ya think I give you a plain, dark business suit to work in?

VAL [*sadly*]: Un-hun. . . . [*Sighs and removes his blue jacket.*]

LADY: Now what're you takin' that off for?

VAL: I'm giving the suit back to you. I'll change my pants in the closet. [*Gives her the jacket and crosses into alcove.*]

LADY: Hey! I'm sorry! You hear me? I didn't sleep well last

night. Hey! I said I'm sorry! You hear me? [*She enters alcove and returns immediately with Val's guitar and crosses downstage. He follows.*]

VAL: Le' me have my guitar, Lady. You find too many faults with me and I tried to do good.

LADY: I told you I'm sorry. You want me to get down and lick the dust off your shoes?

VAL: Just give me back my guitar.

LADY: I ain't dissatisfied with you. I'm pleased with you, sincerely!

VAL: You sure don't show it.

LADY: My nerves are all shot to pieces. [*Extends hand to him.*] Shake.

VAL: You mean I ain't fired, so I don't have to quit? [*They shake hands like two men. She hands him guitar—then silence falls between them.*]

LADY: You see, we don't know each other, we're, we're—just gettin'—acquainted.

VAL: That's right, like a couple of animals sniffin' around each other. . . .

[*The image embarrasses her. He crosses to counter, leans over and puts guitar behind it.*]

LADY: Well, not exactly like that, but—!

VAL: We don't know each other. How do people get to know each other? I used to think they did it by touch.

LADY: By what?

VAL: By touch, by touchin' each other.

LADY [*moving up and sitting on shoe-fitting chair which has been moved to right window*]: Oh, you mean by close—contact!

VAL: But later it seemed like that made them more strangers than ever, uhh, huh, more strangers than ever. . . .

LADY: Then how d'you think they get to know each other?

VAL [*sitting on counter*]: Well, in answer to your last question, I would say this: Nobody ever gets to know *no body!* We're all of us sentenced to solitary confinement inside our own skins, for life! You understand me, Lady? —I'm tellin' you it's the truth, we got to face it, we're under a lifelong sentence to solitary confinement inside our own lonely skins for as long as we live on this earth!

LADY [*rising and crossing to him*]: Oh, no, I'm not a big optimist but I cannot agree with something as sad as that statement!

[*They are sweetly grave as two children; the store is somewhat dusky. She sits in chair right of counter.*]

VAL: Listen! —When I was a kid on Witches Bayou? After my folks all scattered away like loose chicken's feathers blown around by the wind?—I stayed there alone on the bayou, hunted and trapped out of season and hid from the law! —Listen! —All that time, all that lonely time, I felt I was—waiting for something!

LADY: What for?

VAL: What does anyone wait for? For something to happen, for anything to happen, to make things make more sense. . . . It's hard to remember what that feeling was like because I've lost it now, but I was waiting for something like if you ask a question you wait for someone to answer, but you ask the wrong question or you ask the wrong person and the answer don't come. Does every-thing stop because you don't get the answer? No, it goes right on as if the answer was given, day comes after day and night comes after night, and you're still waiting for someone to answer the question and going right on as if the question was answered. And then—well—then. . . .

LADY: Then what?

VAL: You get the make-believe answer.

LADY: What answer is that?

VAL: Don't pretend you don't know because you do!

LADY: —Love?

VAL [*placing hand on her shoulder*]: That's the make-believe answer. It's fooled many a fool besides you an' me, that's the God's truth, Lady, and you had better believe it. [*Lady looks reflectively at Val and he goes on speaking and sits on stool below counter.*] —I met a girl on the bayou when I was fourteen. I'd had a feeling that day that if I just kept poling the boat down the bayou a little bit further I would come bang into whatever it was I'd been so long expecting!

LADY: Was she the answer, this girl that you met on the bayou?

VAL: She made me think that she was.

LADY: How did she do that?

VAL: By coming out on the dogtrot of a cabin as naked as I was in that flat-bottom boat! She stood there a while with the daylight burning around her as bright as heaven as far as I could see. You seen the inside of a shell, how white that is, pearly white? Her naked skin was like that. —Oh, God, I remember a bird flown out of the moss and its wings made a shadow on her, and then it sung a single, high clear note, and as if she was waiting for that as a kind of a signal to catch me, she turned and smiled, and walked on back in the cabin. . . .

LADY: You followed?

VAL: Yes, I followed, I followed, like a bird's tail follows a bird, I followed! I thought that she give me the answer to the question, I'd been waiting for, but afterwards I wasn't sure that was it, but from that time the question wasn't much plainer than the answer and—

LADY: —What?

VAL: At fifteen I left Witches Bayou. When the dog died I sold my boat and the gun. . . . I went to New Orleans in this snakeskin jacket. . . . It didn't take long for me to learn the score.

LADY: What did you learn?

VAL: I learned that I had something to sell besides snakeskins and other wild things' skins I caught on the bayou. I was corrupted! That's the answer. . . .

LADY: Naw, that ain't the answer!

VAL: Okay, *you* tell me the answer!

LADY: I don't know the answer, I just know corruption ain't the answer. I know that much. If I thought that was the answer I'd take Jabe's pistol or his morphine tablets and—

[*A woman bursts into store.*]

WOMAN: I got to use your pay phone!

LADY: Go ahead. Help yourself.

[*Woman crosses to phone, deposits coin. Lady crosses to confectionery. To Val:*]

Get me a coke from the cooler.

[*Val crosses and goes out right. During the intense activity among the choral women, Lady and Val seem bemused, as if they were thinking back over their talk before. For the past minute or two a car horn has been heard blowing repeatedly in the near distance.*]

WOMAN [*at phone*]: Cutrere place, get me the Cutrere place, will yuh? David Cutrere or his wife, whichever comes to the phone!

BEULAH [*rushes in from the street to right-center*]: Lady, Lady, where's Lady! Carol Cutrere is—!

WOMAN: Quiet, please! I am callin' her brother about her!

[*Lady sits at table in confectionery.*]

WOMAN [*at phone*]: Who's this I'm talking to? Good! I'm calling about your sister, Carol Cutrere. She is blowing her car horn at the Red Crown station, she is blowing and blowing her car horn at the Red Crown station because my husband give the station attendants instructions not to service her car, and she is blowing and blowing and blowing on her horn, drawing a big crowd there and, Mr. Cutrere, I thought that you and your father had agreed to keep that girl out of Two River County for good, that's what we all understood around here.

[*Car horn.*]

BEULAH [*listening with excited approval*]: Good! Good! Tell him that if—

[*Dolly enters.*]

DOLLY: She's gotten out of the car and—

BEULAH: *Shhh!*

WOMAN: Well, I just wanted to let you know she's back here in town makin' another disturbance and my husband's on the phone now at the Red Crown station— [*Dolly goes outside and looks off.*] —trying to get the Sheriff, so if she gits picked up again by th' law, you can't say I didn't warn you, Mr. Cutrere. [*Car horn.*]

DOLLY [*coming back in*]: Oh, good! Good!

BEULAH: Where is she, where's she gone now?

WOMAN: You better be quick about it. Yes, I do. I sympathize with you and your father and with Mrs. Cutrere, but Carol cannot demand service at our station, we just refuse to wait on her, she's not—Hello? Hello? [*She jiggles phone violently.*]

BEULAH: What's he doin'? Comin' to pick her up?

DOLLY: Call the Sheriff's office!

[*Beulah goes outside again. Val comes back with a bottle of Coca-Cola—hands it to Lady and leans on juke box.*]

DOLLY [*going out to Beulah*]: What's goin' on now?

BEULAH [*outside*]: Look, look, they're pushing her out of the station driveway.

[*They forget Lady in this new excitement. Ad libs continual. The short woman from the station charges back out of the store.*]

DOLLY: Where is Carol?

BEULAH: Going into the White Star Pharmacy! [*Dolly rushes back in to the phone. Beulah, crossing to Lady.*] Lady, I want you to give me your word that if that Cutrere girl comes in here, you won't wait on her! You hear me?

LADY: No.

BEULAH: —What? Will you refuse to wait on her?

LADY: I can't refuse to wait on anyone in this store.

BEULAH: Well, I'd like to know why you can't.

DOLLY: Shhh! I'm on the phone!

BEULAH: Who you phonin' Dolly?

DOLLY: That White Star Pharmacy! I want to make sure that Mr. Dubinsky refuses to wait on that girl! [*Having found and deposited coin.*] I want the White Far Starmacy. I mean the— [*Stamps foot.*] —White Star Pharmacy! —I'm so upset my tongue's twisted!

[*Lady hands coke to Val. Beulah is at the window.*]

I'm getting a busy signal. Has she come out yet?

BEULAH: No, she's still in the White Star!

DOLLY: Maybe they're not waiting on her.

BEULAH: Dubinsky'd wait on a purple-bottom baboon if it put a dime on th' counter an' pointed at something!

DOLLY: I know she sat at a table in the Blue Bird Café half'n hour last time she was here and the waitresses never came near her!

BEULAH: That's different. They're not foreigners there!

[*Dolly crosses to counter.*]

You can't ostracize a person out of this county unless everybody cooperates. Lady just told me that she was going to wait on her if she comes here.

DOLLY: Lady wouldn't do that.

BEULAH: *Ask* her! She told *me* she would!

LADY [*rising and turning at once to the women and shouting at them*]: Oh, for God's sake, no! I'm not going to refuse to wait on her because you all don't like her! Besides I'm delighted that wild girl is givin' her brother so much trouble! [*After this outburst she goes back of the counter.*]

DOLLY [*at phone*]: Hush! Mr. Dubinsky! This is Dolly Hamma, Mr. "Dog" Hamma's wife!

[*Carol quietly enters the front door.*]

I want to ask you, is Carol Cutrere in your drugstore?

BEULAH [*warningly*]: Dolly!

CAROL: No. She isn't.

DOLLY: —What?

CAROL: She's here.

[*Beulah goes into confectionery. Carol moves toward Val downstage.*]

DOLLY: —Aw! —Never mind, Mr. Dubinsky, I— [*Hangs up furiously and crosses to door.*]

[*A silence in which they all stare at the girl from various positions about the store. She has been on the road all night in an open car: her hair is blown wild, her face flushed and eyes bright with fever. Her manner in the scene is that of a wild animal at bay, desperate but fearless.*]

LADY [*finally and quietly*]: Hello, Carol.

CAROL: Hello, Lady.

LADY [*defiantly cordial*]: I thought that you were in New Orleans, Carol.

CAROL: Yes, I was. Last night.

LADY: Well, you got back fast.

CAROL: I drove all night.

LADY: In that storm?

CAROL: The wind took the top off my car but I didn't stop. [*She watches Val steadily; he steadily ignores her; turns away and puts bottles of Coca-Cola on a table.*]

LADY [*with growing impatience*]: Is something wrong at home, is someone sick?

CAROL [*absently*]: No. No, not that I know of, I wouldn't know if there was, they—may I sit down?

LADY: Why, sure.

CAROL [*crossing to chair at counter and sitting*]: —They pay me to stay away so I wouldn't know. . . .

[*Silence, Val walks deliberately past her and goes into alcove.*]

—I think I have a fever, I feel like I'm catching pneumonia, everything's so far away. . . .

[*Silence again except for the faint, hissing whispers of Beulah and Dolly at the back of the store.*]

LADY [*with a touch of exasperation*]: Is there something you want?

CAROL: Everything seems miles away. . . .

LADY: Carol, I said is there anything you want here?

CAROL: Excuse me!—yes. . . .

LADY: Yes, what?

CAROL: Don't bother now. I'll wait.

[*Val comes out of alcove with the blue jacket on.*]

LADY: Wait for what, what are you waiting for! You don't have to wait for nothing, just say what you want and if I got it in stock I'll give it to you!

[*Phone rings once.*]

CAROL [*vaguely*]: —Thank you—no. . . .

LADY [*to Val*]: Get that phone, Val.

[*Dolly crosses and hisses something inaudible to Beulah.*]

BEULAH [*rising*]: I just want to wait here to see if she does or she don't

DOLLY: She just said she would!

BEULAH: Just the same, I'm gonna wait!!

VAL [*at phone*]: Yes, sir, she is. —I'll tell her. [*Hangs up and speaks to Lady.*] Her brother's heard she's here and he's coming to pick her up.

LADY: *David Cutrere is not coming in this store!*

DOLLY: Aw-aw!

BEULAH: David Cutrere used to be her lover.

DOLLY: I remember you told me.

LADY [*wheels about suddenly toward the women*]: Beulah! Dolly! Why're you back there hissing together like geese? [*Coming from behind counter to right-center.*] Why don't you go to th'—Blue Bird and—have some hot coffee—talk there!

BEULAH: It looks like we're getting what they call the bum's rush.

DOLLY: I never stay where I'm not wanted and when I'm not wanted somewhere I never come back! [*They cross out and slam door.*]

LADY [*after a pause*]: What did you come here for?

CAROL: To deliver a message.

LADY: To me?

CAROL: No.

LADY: Then who?

[*Carol stares at Lady gravely a moment, then turns slowly to look at Val.*]

—Him?—Him?

[*Carol nods slowly and slightly.*]

OK, then, give him the message, deliver the message to him.

CAROL: It's a private message. Could I speak to him alone, please?

[*Lady gets a shawl from a hook.*]

LADY: Oh, for God's sake! Your brother's plantation is ten minutes from here in that sky-blue Cadillac his rich wife give him. Now look, he's on his way here but I won't let him come in, I don't even want his hand to touch the door-handle. I know your message, this boy knows your message, there's nothing private about it. But I tell you, that this boy's not for sale in my store! —Now—I'm going out to watch for the sky-blue Cadillac on the highway. When I see it, I'm going to throw this door open and holler and when I holler, I want you out of this door like a shot from a pistol!—that fast! Understand?

[NOTE: *Above scene is overextended. This can be remedied by a very lively performance. It might also help to indicate a division between the Lady-Val scene and the group scene that follows. Lady slams door behind her. The loud noise of the door-slam increases the silence that follows, Val's oblivious attitude is not exactly hostile, but deliberate. There's a kind of purity in it; also a kind of refusal to concern himself with a problem that isn't his own. He holds his guitar with a specially tender concentration, and strikes a soft chord on it. The girl stares at Val; he whistles a note and tightens a guitar string to the pitch of the whistle, not looking at the girl. Since this scene is followed by the emotional scene between Lady and David, it should be keyed somewhat lower than written; it's important that Val should not seem brutal in his attitude toward Carol; there should be an air between them of two lonely children.*]

VAL [*in a soft, preoccupied tone*]: You told the lady I work for that you had a message for me. Is that right, miss? Have you got a message for me?

CAROL [*she rises, moves a few steps toward him, hesitantly. Val whistles, plucks guitar string, changes pitch*]: You've spilt some ashes on your new blue suit.

VAL: Is that the message?

CAROL [*moves away a step*]: No. No, that was just an excuse to touch you. The message is—

VAL: What?

[*Music fades in—guitar.*]

CAROL: —I'd love to hold something the way you hold your guitar, that's how I'd love to hold something, with such—*tender protection!* I'd love to hold *you* that way, with that same—*tender*

64

protection! [*Her hand has fallen onto his knee, which he has drawn up to rest a foot on the counter stool.*] —*Because you hang the moon for me!*

VAL [*he speaks to her, not roughly but in a tone that holds a long history that began with a romantic acceptance of such declarations as she has just made to him, and that turned gradually to his present distrust. He puts guitar down and goes to her*]: Who're you tryin' t' fool beside you'self? You couldn't stand the weight of a man's body on you. [*He casually picks up her wrist and pushes the sleeve back from it.*] What's this here? A human wrist with a bone? It feels like a twig I could snap with two fingers. . . . [*Gently, negligently, pushes collar of her trench coat back from her bare throat and shoulders. Runs a finger along her neck tracing a vein.*] Little girl, you're transparent, I can see the veins in you. A man's weight on you would break you like a bundle of sticks. . . .

[*Music fades out.*]

CAROL [*gazes at him, startled by his perception*]: Isn't it funny! You've hit on the truth about me. The act of love-making is almost unbearably painful, and yet, of course, I do bear it, because to be not alone, even for a few moments, is worth the pain and the danger. It's dangerous for me because I'm not built for childbearing.

VAL: Well, then, fly away, little bird, fly away before you—get broke. [*He turns back to his guitar.*]

CAROL: Why do you dislike me?

VAL [*turning back*]: I never dislike nobody till they interfere with me.

CAROL: How have I interfered with you? Did I snitch when I saw my cousin's watch on you?

VAL [*Beginning to remove his watch*]: —You won't take my

word for a true thing I told you. I'm thirty years old and I'm done with the crowd you run with and the places you run to. The Club Rendezvous, the Starlite Lounge, the Music Bar, and all the night places. Here— [*Offers watch.*] —take this Rolex Chronometer that tells the time of the day and the day of the week and the month and all the crazy moon's phases. I never stole nothing before. When I stole that I known it was time for me to get off the party, so take it back, now, to Bertie. . . . [*He takes her hand and tries to force the watch into her fist. There is a little struggle, he can't open her fist. She is crying, but staring fiercely into his eyes. He draws a hissing breath and hurls watch violently across the floor.*] —That's my message to you and the pack you run with!

CAROL [*flinging coat away*]: *I RUN WITH NOBODY!* —I hoped I could run with you. . . . [*Music stops short.*] You're in danger here, Snakeskin. You've taken off the jacket that said: "I'm wild, I'm alone!" and put on the nice blue uniform of a convict! . . . Last night I woke up thinking about you again. I drove all night to bring you this warning of danger. . . . [*Her trembling hand covers her lips.*] —The message I came here to give you was a warning of danger! I hoped you'd hear me and let me take you away before it's—too late.

[*Door bursts open. Lady rushes inside, crying out:*]

LADY: *Your brother's coming, go out! He can't come in!*

[*Carol picks up coat and goes into confectionery, sobbing. Val crosses toward door.*]

Lock that door! Don't let him come in my store!

[*Carol sinks sobbing at table. Lady runs up to the landing of the stairs as David Cutrere enters the store. He is a tall man in hunter's clothes. He is hardly less handsome now than he*

*was in his youth but something has gone: his power is that of
a captive who rules over other captives. His face, his eyes, have
something of the same desperate, unnatural hardness that Lady
meets the world with.*]

DAVID: Carol?

VAL: She's in there. [*He nods toward the dim confectionery into
which the girl has retreated.*]

DAVID [*crossing*]: Carol! [*She rises and advances a few steps
into the lighted area of the stage.*] You broke the agreement. [*Carol
nods slightly, staring at Val. Then David, harshly.*] All right. I'll
drive you back. Where's your coat? [*Carol murmurs something
inaudible, staring at Val.*] Where is her coat, where is my sister's
coat?

[*Val crosses below and picks up the coat that Carol has dropped
on the floor and hands it to David. He throws it roughly about
Carol's shoulders and propels her forcefully toward store entrance. Val moves away to downstage right.*]

LADY [*suddenly and sharply*]: Wait, please!

[*David looks up at the landing; stands frozen as Lady rushes
down the stairs.*]

DAVID [*softly, hoarsely*]: How—are you, Lady?

LADY [*turning to Val*]: Val, go out.

DAVID [*to Carol*]: Carol, will you wait for me in my car?

[*He opens the door for his sister; she glances back at Val with
desolation in her eyes. Val crosses quickly through the confectionery. Sound of door closing in there. Carol nods slightly as
if in sad response to some painful question and goes out of the
store. Pause.*]

LADY: I told you once to never come in this store.

DAVID: I came for my sister. . . . [*He turns as if to go.*]

LADY: No, wait!

DAVID: I don't dare leave my sister alone on the road.

LADY: I have something to tell you I never told you before. [*She crosses to him. David turns back to her, then moves away to downstage right-center.*] —I—carried your child in my body the summer you quit me. [*Silence.*]

DAVID: —I—didn't know.

LADY: No, no, I didn't write you no letter about it; I was proud then; I had pride. But I had your child in my body the summer you quit me, that summer they burned my father in his wine garden, and you, you washed your hands clean of any connection with a Dago bootlegger's daughter and— [*Her breathless voice momentarily falters and she makes a fierce gesture as she struggles to speak.*] —took that—society girl that—restored your homeplace and give you such— [*Catches breath.*] —well-born children. . . .

DAVID: —I—didn't know.

LADY: Well, now you do know, you know now. I carried your child in my body the summer you quit me but I had it cut out of my body, and they cut my heart out with it!

DAVID: —I—didn't know.

LADY: I wanted death after that, but death don't come when you *want* it, it comes when you don't want it! I wanted death, then, but I took the next best thing. *You* sold *yourself. I* sold *my*self. *You* was bought. *I* was bought. You made whores of us both!

DAVID: —I—didn't know. . . .

[*Mandolin, barely audible, "Dicitencello Vuoi."*]

LADY: But that's all a long time ago. Some reason I drove by there a few nights ago; the shore of the lake where my father had his wine garden? You remember? You remember the wine garden of my father?

[*David stares at her. She turns away.*]

No, you don't? You don't remember it even?

DAVID: —Lady, I don't—remember—anything else. . . .

LADY: The mandolin of my father, the songs that I sang with my father in my father's wine garden?

DAVID: Yes, I don't remember anything else. . . .

LADY: *Core Ingrata! Come Le Rose!* And we disappeared and he would call, *"Lady? Lady?"* [*Turns to him.*] *How could I answer him with two tongues in my mouth!* [*A sharp hissing intake of breath, eyes opened wide, hand clapped over her mouth as if what she said was unendurable to her. He turns instantly, sharply away. Music stops short, Jabe begins to knock for her on the floor above. She crosses to stairs, stops, turns.*] I hold hard feelings! —Don't ever come here again. If your wild sister comes here, send somebody else for her, not you, not you. Because I hope never to feel this knife again in me. [*Her hand is on her chest; she breathes with difficulty.*]

[*He turns away from her; starts toward the door. She takes a step toward him.*]

And don't pity me neither. I haven't gone down so terribly far in the world. I got a going concern in this mercantile store, in there's the confectionery which'll reopen this spring, it's being done over to make it the place that all the young people will come to, it's going to be like—

[*He touches the door, pauses with his back to her.*]

—the wine garden of my father, those wine-drinking nights when you had something better than anything you've had since!

DAVID: Lady—*That's*—

LADY: —*What?*

DAVID: —*True!* [*Opens door.*]

LADY: Go now. I just wanted to tell you my life ain't over.

[*He goes out as Jabe continues knocking. She stands, stunned, motionless till Val quietly re-enters the store. She becomes aware of his return rather slowly; then she murmurs.*]

I made a fool of myself. . . .

VAL: What?

[*She crosses to stairs.*]

LADY: *I made a fool of myself!* [*She goes up the stairs with effort as the lights change slowly to mark a division of scenes.*]

Sunset of that day. Val is alone in the store, as if preparing to go. The sunset is fiery. A large woman opens the door and stands there looking dazed. It is Vee Talbott.

VAL [*turning*]: Hello, Mrs. Talbott.

VEE: Something's gone wrong with my eyes. I can't see nothing.

VAL [*going to her*]: Here, let me help you. You probably drove up here with that setting sun in your face. [*Leading her to shoe-fitting chair at right window.*] There now. Set down right here.

VEE: Thank you—so—much. . . .

VAL: I haven't seen you since that night you brought me here to ask for this job.

VEE: Has the minister called on you yet? Reverend Tooker? I made him promise he would. I told him you were new around here and weren't affiliated to any church yet. I want you to go to ours.

VAL: —That's—mighty kind of you.

VEE: The Church of the Resurrection, it's Episcopal.

VAL: Uh, huh.

VEE: Unwrap that picture, please.

VAL: Sure. [*He tears paper off canvas.*]

VEE: It's the Church of the Resurrection. I give it a sort of imaginative treatment. You know, Jabe and Lady have never darkened a church door. I thought it ought to be hung where Jabe could look at it, it might help to bring that poor dying man to Jesus. . . .

[*Val places it against chair right of counter and crouches before the canvas, studying it long and seriously, Vee coughs nervously, gets up, bends to look at the canvas, sits uncertainly back down. Val smiles at her warmly, then back to the canvas.*]

VAL [*at last*]: What's this here in the picture?

VEE: The steeple.

VAL: Aw. —Is the church steeple red?

VEE: Why—no, but—

VAL: Why'd you paint it red, then?

VEE: Oh, well, you see, I— [*Laughs nervously, childlike in her growing excitement.*] —I just, just *felt* it that way! I paint a thing how I feel it instead of always the way it actually is. Appearances are misleading, nothing is what it looks like to the eyes. You got to have—*vision—to see!*

VAL: —Yes. Vision. Vision!—to see. . . . [*Rises, nodding gravely, emphatically.*]

VEE: I paint from vision. They call me a visionary.

VAL: Oh.

VEE [*with shy pride*]: That's what the New Orleans and Memphis newspaper people admire so much in my work. They call it a primitive style, the work of a visionary. One of my pictures is hung on the exhibition in Audubon Park museum and they have asked for others. I can't turn them out fast enough! —I have to wait for—visions, no, I—I can't paint without—visions . . . I couldn't *live* without visions!

VAL: Have you always had visions?

VEE: No, just since I was born, I— [*Stops short, startled by the absurdity of her answer. Both laugh suddenly, then she rushes on, her great bosom heaving with curious excitement, twisting in her chair, gesturing with clenched hands.*] I was born, I was born with a caul! A sort of thing like a veil, a thin, thin sort of a web was over my eyes. They call that a caul. It's a sign that you're going to have visions, and I did, I had them! [*Pauses for breath; light fades.*] —When I was little my baby sister died. Just one day old, she died. They had to baptize her at midnight to save her soul.

VAL: Uh-huh. [*He sits opposite her, smiling, attentive.*]

VEE: The minister came at midnight, and after the baptism service, he handed the bowl of holy water to me and told me, "Be sure to empty this out on the ground!"—I didn't. I was scared to go out at midnight, with, with—death! in the—house and—I sneaked into the kitchen; I emptied the holy water into the kitchen sink—thunder struck! —the kitchen sink turned black, the kitchen sink turned absolutely black!

[*Sheriff Talbott enters the front door.*]

TALBOTT: Mama! What're you doin?

VEE: Talkin'.

TALBOTT: I'm gonna see Jabe a minute, you go out and wait in th' car. [*He goes up. She rises slowly, picks up canvas and moves to counter.*]

VEE: —Oh, I—tell you!—since I got into this painting, my whole outlook is different. I can't explain how it is, the difference to me.

VAL: You don't have to explain. I know what you mean. Before you started to paint, it didn't make sense.

VEE: —What—what didn't?

VAL: Existence!

VEE [*slowly and softly*]: No—no, it didn't . . . existence didn't make sense. . . . [*She places canvas on guitar on counter and sits in chair.*]

VAL [*rising and crossing to her*]: You lived in Two River County, the wife of the county sheriff. You saw awful things take place.

VEE: Awful! Things!

VAL: Beatings!

VEE: Yes!

VAL: Lynchings!

VEE: Yes!

VAL: Runaway convicts torn to pieces by hounds!

[*This is the first time she could express this horror.*]

VEE: *Chain-gang dogs!*

VAL: Yeah?

VEE: Tear fugitives!

VAL: Yeah?

VEE: —to *pieces.* . . .

[*She had half risen: now sinks back faintly. Val looks beyond her in the dim store, his light eyes have a dark gaze. It may be that his speech is too articulate: counteract this effect by groping, hesitations.*]

VAL [*moving away a step*]: But violence ain't quick always. Sometimes it's slow. Some tornadoes are slow. Corruption—rots men's hearts and—rot is slow. . . .

VEE: —How do you—?

VAL: Know? I been a witness, I know!

VEE: *I* been a witness! *I* know!

VAL: We seen these things from seats down front at the show. [*He crouches before her and touches her hands in her lap. Her breath shudders*] And so you begun to paint your visions. Without no plan, no training, you started to paint as if God touched your fingers. [*He lifts her hands slowly, gently from her soft lap.*] You made some beauty out of this dark country with these two, soft, woman hands. . . . [*Talbott appears on the stair landing, looks down, silent.*] Yeah, you made some beauty! [*Strangely, gently, he lifts her hands to his mouth. She gasps. Talbott calls out:*]

TALBOTT: *Hey!* [*Vee springs up, gasping. Talbott descending.*] *Cut this crap!* [*Val moves away to right-center. Talbott to Vee.*] Go out. Wait in the car. [*He stares at Val till Vee lumbers out as if dazed. After a while:*] Jabe Torrance told me to take a good look at you. [*Crosses to Val.*] Well, now, I've taken that look. [*Nods shortly. Goes out of store. The store is now very dim. As door closes on Talbott, Val picks up painting; he goes behind counter and places it on a shelf, then picks up his guitar and sits on counter. Lights go down to mark a division as he sings and plays "Heavenly Grass."*]

As Val finishes the song, Lady descends the stair. He rises and turns on a green-shaded light bulb.

VAL [*to Lady*]: You been up there a long time.

LADY: —I gave him morphine. He must be out of his mind. He says such awful things to me. He says I want him to die.

VAL: You sure you don't?

LADY: I don't want no one to die. Death's terrible, Val. [*Pause. She wanders to right front window. He takes his guitar and crosses to the door.*] You gotta go now?

VAL: I'm late.

LADY: Late for what? You got a date with somebody?

VAL: —No. . . .

LADY: Then stay a while. Play something. I'm all unstrung. . . . [*He crosses back and leans against counter; the guitar is barely audible, under the speeches.*] I made a terrible fool of myself down here today with—

VAL: —That girl's brother?

LADY: Yes, I—threw away——pride. . . .

VAL: His sister said she'd come here to give me a warning. I wonder what of?

LADY [*sitting in shoe-fitting chair*]: —I said things to him I should of been too proud to say. . . .

[*Both are pursuing their own reflections; guitar continues softly.*]

VAL: Once or twice lately I've woke up with a fast heart, shouting something, and had to pick up my guitar to calm myself down. . . . Somehow or other I can't get used to this place, I don't feel safe in this place, but I—want to stay. . . . [*Stops short; sound of wild baying.*]

LADY: The chain-gang dogs are chasing some runaway convict. . . .

VAL: *Run boy! Run fast, brother! If they catch you, you never will run again! That's—* [*He has thrust his guitar under his arm on this line and crossed to the door.*] —for sure. . . . [*The baying of the dogs changes, becomes almost a single savage note.*] —Uh-huh—the dogs've got him. . . . [*Pause.*] They're tearing him to pieces! [*Pause. Baying continues. A shot is fired. The baying dies out. He stops with his hand on the door; glances back at her; nods; draws the door open. The wind sings loud in the dusk.*]

LADY: *Wait!*

VAL: —Huh?

LADY: —Where do you stay?

VAL: —When?

LADY: Nights.

VAL: I stay at the Wildwood cabins on the highway.

LADY: You like it there?

VAL: Uh-huh.

LADY: —Why?

VAL: I got a comfortable bed, a two-burner stove, a shower and icebox there.

LADY: You want to save money?

VAL: I never could in my life.

LADY: You could if you stayed on the place.

VAL: What place?

LADY: This place.

VAL: Whereabouts on this place?

LADY [*pointing to alcove*]: Back of that curtain.

VAL: —Where they try on clothes?

LADY: There's a cot there. A nurse slept on it when Jabe had his first operation, and there's a washroom down here and I'll get a plumber to put in a hot an' cold shower! I'll—fix it up nice for you. . . . [*She rises, crosses to foot of stairs. Pause. He lets the door shut, staring at her.*]

VAL [*moving downstage center*]: —I—don't like to be—obligated.

LADY: There wouldn't be no obligation, you'd do me a favor. I'd feel safer at night with somebody on the place. I would; it would cost you nothing! And you could save up that money you spend on the cabin. How much? Ten a week? Why, two or three months from now you'd—save enough money to— [*Makes a wide gesture with a short laugh as if startled.*] Go on! Take a look at it! See if it don't suit you! —All right. . . .

[*But he doesn't move; he appears reflective.*]

LADY [*shivering, hugging herself*]: Where does heat go in this building?

VAL [*reflectively*]: —Heat rises. . . .

LADY: You with your dog's temperature, don't feel cold, do you? I do! I turn blue with it!

VAL: —Yeah. . . .

[*The wait is unendurable to Lady.*]

LADY: *Well, aren't you going to look at it, the room back there, and see if it suits you or not?!*

VAL: —*I'll go and take a look at it. . . . [He crosses to the alcove and disappears behind the curtain. A light goes on behind it, making its bizarre pattern translucent: a gold tree with scarlet fruit and white birds in it, formally designed. Truck roars; lights sweep the frosted window, Lady gasps aloud; takes out a pint bottle and a glass from under the counter, setting them down with a crash that makes her utter a startled exclamation: then a startled laugh. She pours a drink and sits in chair right of counter. The lights turn off behind alcove curtain and Val comes back out. She sits stiffly without looking at him as he crosses back lazily, goes behind counter, puts guitar down. His manner is gently sad as if he had met with a familiar, expected disappointment. He sits down quietly on edge of counter and takes the pint bottle and pours himself a shot of the liquor with a reflective sigh. Boards creak loudly, contracting with the cold, Lady's voice is harsh and sudden, demanding:]*

LADY: *Well, is it okay or—what!*

VAL: I never been in a position where I could turn down something I got for nothing in my life. I like that picture in there. That's a famous picture, that "September Morn" picture you got on the wall in there. Ha ha! I might have trouble sleeping in a room with that picture. I might keep turning the light on to take another look at it! The way she's cold in that water and sort of crouched over in it, holding her body like that, that—might—ha ha!—sort of keep me awake. . . .

LADY: Aw, you with your dog's temperature and your control of all functions, it would take more than a picture to keep you awake!

VAL: I was just kidding.

LADY: I was just kidding too.

VAL: But you know how a single man is. He don't come home every night with just his shadow.

[*Pause. She takes a drink.*]

LADY: You bring girls home nights to the Wildwood cabins, do you?

VAL: I ain't so far. But I would like to feel free to. That old life is what I'm used to. I always worked nights in cities and if you work nights in cities you live in a different city from those that work days.

LADY: Yes. I know, I—imagine. . . .

VAL: The ones that work days in cities and the ones that work nights in cities, they live in different cities. The cities have the same name but they are different cities. As different as night and day. There's something wild in the country that only the night people know. . . .

LADY: Yeah, I know!

VAL: I'm thirty years old!—but sudden changes don't work, it takes—

LADY: —Time—yes. . . . [*Slight pause which she finds disconcerting. He slides off counter and moves around below it.*]

VAL: You been good to me, Lady. —Why d'you want me to stay here?

LADY [*defensively*]: I told you why.

VAL: For company nights?

LADY: Yeah, to, to!—*guard the store,* nights!

VAL: To be a night watchman?

LADY: Yeah, to be a night *watchman.*

VAL: You feel nervous alone here?

LADY: Naturally now! —Jabe sleeps with a pistol next to him but if somebody broke in the store, he couldn't git up and all I could do is holler! —Who'd *hear* me? They got a telephone girl on the night shift with—sleepin' sickness, I think! Anyhow, why're you so suspicious? You look at me like you thought I was *plottin.* —Kind people *exist:* Even me! [*She sits up rigid in chair, lips and eyes tight closed, drawing in a loud breath which comes from a tension both personal and vicarious.*]

VAL: I understand, Lady, but. . . . Why're you sitting up so stiff in that chair?

LADY: Ha! [*Sharp laugh; she leans back in chair.*]

VAL: You're still unrelaxed.

LADY: I know.

VAL: Relax. [*Moving around close to her.*] I'm going to show you some tricks I learned from a lady osteopath that took me in, too.

LADY: What tricks?

VAL: How to manipulate joints and bones in a way that makes you feel like a loose piece of string. [*Moves behind her chair. She watches him.*] Do you trust me or don't you?

LADY: Yeah, I trust you completely, but—

VAL: Well then, lean forward a little and raise your arms up and turn sideways in the chair.

[*She follows these instructions.*]

Drop your head. [*He manipulates her head and neck.*] Now the spine, Lady. [*He places his knee against the small of her backbone and she utters a sharp, startled laugh as he draws her backbone hard against his kneecap.*]

LADY: Ha, ha! —That makes a sound like, like, like! —boards contracting with cold in the building, ha, ha!

[*She relaxes.*]

VAL: Better?

LADY: Oh, yes!—much . . . thanks. . . .

VAL [*stroking her neck*]: Your skin is like silk. You're light skinned to be Italian.

LADY: Most people in this country think Italian people are dark. Some are but not all are! Some of them are fair . . very fair. . . . My father's people were dark but my mother's people were fair. Ha ha!

[*The laughter is senseless. He smiles understandingly at her as she chatters to cover confusion. He turns away, then goes above and sits on counter close to her.*]

My mother's mother's sister—come here from Monte Cassino, to die, with relations! —but I think people always die alone . . . with or without relations. I was a little girl then and I remember it took her such a long, long time to die we almost forgot her. — And she was so quiet . . . in a corner. . . . And I remember asking her one time, Zia Teresa, how does it feel to die? —Only a little girl would ask such a question, ha ha! Oh, and I remember her answer. She said—"It's a lonely feeling." I think she wished she had stayed in Italy and died in a place that she knew. . . . [*Looks at him directly for the first time since mentioning the alcove.*] Well, there is a washroom, and I'll get the plumber to put in a hot and cold shower! Well— [*Rises, retreats awkwardly from the chair. His interest seems to have wandered from her.*] I'll go up and get some clean linen and make up that bed in there.

[*She turns and walks rapidly, almost running, to stairs. He appears lost in some private reflection but as soon as she has disappeared above the landing, he says something under his breath and crosses directly to the cashbox. He coughs loudly to cover the sound of ringing it open; scoops out a fistful of bills and coughs again to cover the sound of slamming drawer shut. Picks up his guitar and goes out the front door of store, Lady returns downstairs, laden with linen. The outer darkness moans through the door left open. She crosses to the door and a little outside it, peering both ways down the dark road. Then she comes in furiously, with an Italian curse, shutting the door with her foot or shoulder, and throws the linen down on counter. She crosses abruptly to cashbox, rings it open and discovers theft. Slams drawer violently shut.*]

Thief! Thief!

[*Turns to phone, lifts receiver. Holds it a moment, then slams it back into place. Wanders desolately back to the door, opens it and stands staring out into the starless night as the scene dims out. Music: blues—guitar.*]

SCENE FOUR

Late that night, Val enters the store, a little unsteadily, with his guitar; goes to the cashbox and rings it open. He counts some bills off a big wad and returns them to the cashbox and the larger wad to the pocket of his snakeskin jacket. Sudden footsteps above; light spills onto stair landing. He quickly moves away from the cashbox as Lady appears on the landing in a white sateen robe; she carries a flashlight.

LADY: Who's that?

[*Music fades out.*]

VAL: —Me.

[*She turns the flashlight on his figure.*]

LADY: Oh, my God, how you scared me!

VAL: You didn't expect me?

LADY: How'd I know it was you I heard come in?

VAL: I thought you give me a room here.

LADY: You left without letting me know if you took it or not. [*She is descending the stairs into store, flashlight still on him.*]

VAL: Catch me turning down something I get for nothing.

LADY: Well, you might have said something so I'd expect you or not.

VAL: I thought you took it for granted.

LADY: I don't take nothing for granted.

[*He starts back to the alcove.*]

Wait! —I'm coming downstairs.... [*She descends with the flashlight beam on his face.*]

VAL: You're blinding me with that flashlight. [*He laughs. She keeps the flashlight on him. He starts back again toward the alcove.*]

LADY: The bed's not made because I didn't expect you.

VAL: That's all right.

LADY: I brought the linen downstairs and you'd cut out.

VAL: —Yeah, well—

[*She picks up linen on counter.*]

Give me that stuff. I can make up my own rack. Tomorrow you'll have to get yourself a new clerk. [*Takes it from her and goes again toward alcove.*] I had a lucky night. [*Exhibits a wad of bills.*]

LADY: *Hey!*

[*He stops near the curtain. She goes and turns on green-shaded bulb over cash box.*]

—*Did you just open this cashbox?*

VAL: —Why you ask that?

LADY: I thought I heard it ring open a minute ago, that's why I come down here.

VAL: —In your—white satin—kimona?

LADY: *Did you just open the cashbox?!*

VAL: —I wonder who did if I didn't. . . .

LADY: Nobody did if you didn't, but somebody did! [*Opens cashbox and hurriedly counts money. She is trembling violently.*]

VAL: How come you didn't lock the cash up in the safe this evening, Lady?

LADY: Sometimes I forget to.

VAL: That's careless.

LADY: —Why'd you open the cashbox when you come in?

VAL: I opened it twice this evening, once before I went out and again when I come back. I borrowed some money and put it back in the box an' got all this left over! [*Shows her the wad of bills.*] I beat a blackjack dealer five times straight. With this much loot I can retire for the season. . . . [*He returns money to pocket.*]

LADY: *Chicken feed!* —I'm sorry for you.

VAL: You're sorry for me?

LADY: I'm sorry for you because nobody can help you. I was touched by your—strangeness, your strange talk. —That thing about birds with no feet so they have to sleep on the wind? —I said to myself, "This boy is a bird with no feet so he has to sleep on the wind," and that softened my fool Dago heart and I wanted to help you. . . . Fool, me! —I got what I should of expected. You robbed me while I was upstairs to get sheets to make up your bed!

[*He starts out toward the door.*]

I guess I'm a fool to even feel disappointed.

VAL [*stopping center and dropping linen on counter*]: You're disappointed in me. I was disappointed in you.

LADY [*coming from behind counter*]: —How did I disappoint you?

VAL: There wasn't no cot behind that curtain before. You put it back there for a purpose.

LADY: It was back there!—folded behind the mirror.

VAL: It wasn't back of no mirror when you told me three times to go and—

LADY [*cutting in*]: I left that money in the cashbox on purpose, to find out if I could trust you.

VAL: You got back th' . . .

LADY: No, no, no, I can't trust you, now I know I can't trust you, I got to trust anybody or I don't want him.

VAL: That's okay, I don't expect no character reference from you.

LADY: I'll give you a character reference. I'd say this boy's a peculiar talker! But I wouldn't say a real hard worker or honest. I'd say a peculiar slew-footer that sweet talks you while he's got his hand in the cashbox.

VAL: I took out less than you owed me.

LADY: Don't mix up the issue. I see through you, mister!

VAL: I see through you, Lady.

LADY: What d'you see through me?

VAL: You sure you want me to tell?

LADY: I'd love for you to.

VAL: —A not so young and not so satisfied woman, that hired a man off the highway to do double duty without paying overtime for it. . . . I mean a store clerk days and a stud nights, and—

LADY: God, no! You—! [*She raises her hand as if to strike at him.*] Oh, God no . . . you cheap little— [*Invectives fail her so she uses her fists, hammering at him with them. He seizes her wrists. She struggles a few moments more, then collapses, in chair, sobbing. He lets go of her gently.*]

VAL: It's natural. You felt—lonely. . . .

[*She sobs brokenly against the counter.*]

LADY: Why did you come back here?

VAL: To put back the money I took so you wouldn't remember me as not honest or grateful— [*He picks up his guitar and starts to the door nodding gravely. She catches her breath; rushes to intercept him, spreading her arms like a crossbar over the door.*]

LADY: NO, NO, DON'T GO . . . I NEED YOU!!!

[*He faces her for five beats. The true passion of her outcry touches him then, and he turns about and crosses to the alcove. . . . As he draws the curtain across it he looks back at her.*]

TO LIVE. . . . TO GO ON LIVING!!!

[*Music fades in—"Lady's Love Song"—guitar. He closes the curtain and turns on the light behind it, making it translucent. Through an opening in the alcove entrance, we see him sitting down with his guitar. Lady picks up the linen and crosses to the alcove like a spellbound child. Just outside it she stops, frozen with uncertainty, a conflict of feelings, but then he begins to whisper the words of a song so tenderly that she is able to draw the curtain open and enter the alcove. He looks up gravely at her from his guitar. She closes the curtain behind her. Its bizarre design, a gold tree with white birds and scarlet fruit in it, is softly translucent with the bulb lighted behind it. The guitar continues softly for a few moments; stops; the stage darkens till only the curtain of the alcove is clearly visible.*]

CURTAIN

An early morning. The Saturday before Easter. The sleeping alcove is lighted. Val is smoking, half dressed, on the edge of the cot. Lady comes running, panting downstairs, her hair loose, in dressing robe and slippers and calls out in a panicky, shrill whisper.

LADY: Val! Val, he's comin' downstairs!

VAL [*hoarse with sleep*]: Who's—what?

LADY: Jabe!

VAL: Jabe?

LADY: I swear he is, he's coming downstairs!

VAL: What of it?

LADY: Jesus, will you get up and put some clothes on? The damned nurse told him that he could come down in the store to check over the stock! You want him to catch you half dressed on that bed there?

VAL: Don't he know I sleep here?

LADY: Nobody knows you sleep here but you and me.

[*Voices above.*]

Oh, God!—they've started.

NURSE: Don't hurry now. Take one step at a time.

[*Footsteps on stairs, slow, shuffling. The professional, nasal cheer of a nurse's voice.*]

LADY [*panicky*]: Get your shirt on! Come out!

NURSE: That's right. One step at a time, one step at a time, lean on my shoulder and take one step at a time.

[*Val rises, still dazed from sleep. Lady gasps and sweeps the curtain across the alcove just a moment before the descending figures enter the sight lines on the landing. Lady breathes like an exhausted runner as she backs away from the alcove and assumes a forced smile. Jabe and the nurse, Miss Porter, appear on the landing of the stairs and at the same moment scudding clouds expose the sun. A narrow window on the landing admits a brilliant shaft of light upon the pair. They have a bizarre and awful appearance, the tall man, his rusty black suit hanging on him like an empty sack, his eyes burning malignantly from his yellow face, leaning on a stumpy little woman with bright pink or orange hair, clad all in starched white, with a voice that purrs with the faintly contemptuous cheer and sweetness of those hired to care for the dying.*]

NURSE: Aw, now, just look at that, that nice bright sun comin' out.

LADY: Miss Porter? It's—it's cold down here!

JABE: What's she say?

NURSE: She says it's cold down here.

LADY: The—the—the air's not warm enough yet, the air's not heated!

NURSE: He's determined to come right down, Mrs. Torrance.

LADY: I know but—

NURSE: Wild horses couldn't hold him a minute longer.

JABE [*exhausted*]: —Let's—rest here a minute. . . .

LADY [*eagerly*]: Yes! Rest there a minute!

NURSE: Okay. We'll rest here a minute. . . .

[*They sit down side by side on a bench under the artificial palm tree in the shaft of light, Jabe glares into the light like a fierce dying old beast. There are sounds from the alcove. To cover them up, Lady keeps making startled, laughing sounds in her throat, half laughing, half panting, chafing her hands together at the foot of the stairs, and coughing falsely.*]

JABE: Lady, what's wrong? Why are you so excited?

LADY: It seems like a miracle to me.

JABE: What seems like a miracle to you?

LADY: You coming downstairs.

JABE: You never thought I would come downstairs again?

LADY: Not this quick! Not as quick as this, Jabe! Did you think he would pick up as quick as this, Miss Porter?

[*Jabe rises.*]

NURSE: Ready?

JABE: Ready.

NURSE: He's doing fine, knock wood.

LADY: Yes, knock wood, knock wood! [*Drums counter loudly with her knuckles. Val steps silently from behind the alcove curtain as the Nurse and Jabe resume their slow, shuffling descent of the stairs. Lady moves back to downstage right-center.*] You got to be careful not to overdo. You don't want another setback. Ain't that right, Miss Porter?

NURSE: Well, it's my policy to mobilize the patient.

LADY [*to Val in a shrill whisper*]: Coffee's boiling, take the goddamn coffeepot off the burner! [*She gives Val a panicky signal to go in the alcove.*]

JABE: Who're you talking to, Lady?

LADY: To—to—to Val, the clerk! I told him to—get you a—chair!

JABE: Who's that?

LADY: Val, Val, the clerk, you know Val!

JABE: Not yet. I'm anxious to meet him. Where is he?

LADY: Right here, right here, here's Val!

[*Val returns from the alcove.*]

JABE: He's here bright and early.

LADY: The early bird catches the worm!

JABE: That's right. Where is the worm?

LADY [*loudly*]: Ha ha!

NURSE: Careful! One step at a time, Mr. Torrance.

LADY: Saturday before Easter's our biggest sales day of the year, I mean second biggest, but sometimes it's even bigger than Christmas Eve! So I told Val to get here a half hour early.

[*Jabe misses his step and stumbles to foot of stairs. Lady screams, Nurse rushes down to him. Val advances and raises the man to his feet.*]

VAL: Here. Here.

LADY: Oh, my God.

NURSE: Oh, oh!

JABE: I'm all right.

NURSE: Are you sure?

LADY: Are you sure?

JABE: Let me go! [*He staggers to lean against counter, panting, glaring, with a malignant smile.*]

LADY: Oh, my God. Oh, my—God. . . .

JABE: This is the boy that works here?

LADY: Yes, this is the clerk I hired to help us out, Jabe.

JABE: How is he doing?

LADY: Fine, fine.

JABE: He's mighty good looking. Do women give him much trouble?

LADY: When school lets out the high-school girls are thick as flies in this store!

JABE: How about older women? Don't he attract older women? The older ones are the buyers, they got the money. They sweat it out of their husbands and throw it away! What's your salary, boy, how much do I pay you?

LADY: Twenty-two fifty a week.

JABE: You're getting him cheap.

VAL: I *get*—commissions.

JABE: Commissions?

VAL: Yes. One percent of all sales.

JABE: Oh? Oh? I didn't know about that.

LADY: I knew he would bring in trade and he brings it in.

JABE: I bet.

LADY: Val, get Jabe a chair, he ought to sit down.

JABE: No, I don't want to sit down. I want to take a look at the new confectionery.

LADY: Oh, yes, yes! Take a look at it! Val, Val, turn on the lights in the confectionery! I want Jabe to see the way I done it over! I'm—real—*proud!*

[*Val crosses and switches on light in confectionery. The bulbs in the arches and the juke box light up.*]

Go in and look at it, Jabe. I am real proud of it!

[*He stares at Lady a moment; then shuffles slowly into the spectral radiance of the confectionery. Lady moves downstage center. At the same time a calliope becomes faintly audible and slowly but steadily builds, Miss Porter goes with the patient, holding his elbow.*]

VAL [*returning to Lady*]: He looks like death.

LADY [*moving away from him*]: *Hush!*

[*Val goes up above counter and stands in the shadows.*]

NURSE: Well, isn't this artistic.

JABE: Yeh. Artistic as hell.

NURSE: I'never seen anything like it before.

JABE: Nobody else did either.

NURSE [*coming back to upstage right-center*]: Who done these decorations?

LADY [*defiantly*]: I did them, all by myself!

NURSE: What do you know. It sure is something artistic.

[*Calliope is now up loud.*]

JABE [*coming back to downstage right*]: Is there a circus or carnival in the county?

LADY: What?

JABE: That sounds like a circus calliope on the highway.

LADY: That's no circus calliope. It's advertising the gala opening of the Torrance Confectionery tonight!

JABE: Doing what did you say?

LADY: It's announcing the opening of our confectionery, it's going all over Glorious Hill this morning and all over Sunset and Lyon this afternoon. Hurry on here so you can see it go by the store. [*She rushes excitedly to open the front door as the ragtime music of the calliope approaches.*]

JABE: I married a live one, Miss Porter. How much does that damn thing cost me?

LADY: You'll be surprised how little. [*She is talking with an hysterical vivacity now.*] I hired it for a song!

JABE: How much of a song did you hire it for?

LADY [*closing door*]: Next to nothing, seven-fifty an hour! And it covers three towns in Two River County!

[*Calliope fades out.*]

JABE [*with a muted ferocity*]: Miss Porter, I married a live one! Didn't I marry a live one? [*Switches off lights in confectionery.*] Her daddy "The Wop" was just as much of a live one till he burned up. [*Lady gasps as if struck. Jabe, with a slow, ugly grin:*] He had a wine garden on the north shore of Moon Lake. The new confectionery sort of reminds me of it. But he made a mistake, he made a bad mistake, one time, selling liquor to niggers. We burned him out. We burned him out, house and orchard and vines and "The Wop" was burned up trying to fight the fire. [*He turns.*] I think I better go up.

LADY: —Did you say "WE"?

JABE: —I have a kind of a cramp. . . .

NURSE [*taking his arm*]: Well, let's go up.

JABE: —Yes, I better go up. . . .

[*They cross to stairs. Calliope fades in.*]

LADY [*almost shouting as she moves downstage center*]: Jabe, did you say "WE" did it, did you say "WE" did it?

JABE [*at foot of stairs, stops, turns*]: Yes, I said "*We*" did it. You heard me, Lady.

NURSE: One step at a time, one step at a time, take it easy.

[*They ascend gradually to the landing and above. The calliope passes directly before the store and a clown is seen, or heard, shouting through megaphone.*]

CLOWN: Don't forget tonight, folks, the gala opening of the Torrance Confectionery, free drinks and free favors, don't forget it, the gala opening of the confectionery.

[*Fade. Jabe and the Nurse disappear above the landing. Calliope gradually fades. A hoarse cry above. The Nurse runs back downstairs, exclaiming:*]

NURSE: He's bleeding, he's having a hemm'rhage! [*Runs to phone.*] Dr. Buchanan's office! [*Turns again to Lady.*] Your husband is having a hemm'rhage!

[*Calliope is loud still. Lady appears not to hear. She speaks to Val.*]

LADY: Did you hear what he said? He said "We" did it, "WE" burned—house—vines—orchard—"The Wop" burned fighting the fire. . . .

[*The scene dims out; calliope fades out.*]

Sunset of the same day. At rise Val is alone. He is standing stock-still down center stage, almost beneath the proscenium, in the tense, frozen attitude of a wild animal listening to something that warns it of danger, his head turned as if he were looking off stage left, out over the house, frowning slightly, attentively. After a moment he mutters something sharply, and his body relaxes; he takes out a cigarette and crosses to the store entrance, opens the door and stands looking out. It has been raining steadily and will rain again in a while, but right now it is clearing: the sun breaks through, suddenly, with great brilliance; and almost at the same instant, at some distance, a woman cries out a great hoarse cry of terror and exaltation; the cry is repeated as she comes running nearer.

Vee Talbott appears through the window as if blind and demented, stiff, groping gestures, shielding her eyes with one arm as she feels along the store window for the entrance, gasping for breath. Val steps aside, taking hold of her arm to guide her into the store. For a few moments she leans weakly, blindly panting for breath against the oval glass of the door, then calls out.

VEE: I'm—*struck blind!*

VAL: You can't see?

VEE: —No! Nothing. . . .

VAL [*assisting her to stool below counter*]: Set down here, Mrs. Talbott.

VEE: —Where?

VAL [*pushing her gently*]: Here. [*Vee sinks moaning onto stool.*] What hurt your eyes, Mrs. Talbott, what happened to your eyes?

VEE [*drawing a long, deep breath*]: The vision I waited and prayed for all my life long!

VAL: You had a vision?

VEE: I saw the eyes of my Savior! —They struck me blind. [*Leans forward, clasping her eyes in anguish.*] Ohhhh, they burned out my eyes!

VAL: Lean back.

VEE: Eyeballs burn like fire. . . .

VAL [*going off right*]: I'll get you something cold to put on your eyes.

VEE: I knew a vision was coming, oh, I had many signs!

VAL [*in confectionery*]: It must be a terrible shock to have a vision. . . . [*He speaks gravely, gently, scooping chipped ice from the soft-drink cooler and wrapping it in his handkerchief.*]

VEE [*with the naïveté of a child, as Val comes back to her*]: I *thought* I would see my Savior on the day of His passion, which was yesterday, Good Friday, that's when I expected to see Him. But I was mistaken, I was—disappointed. Yesterday passed and nothing, nothing much happened but—today— [*Val places handkerchief over her eyes.*] —this afternoon, somehow I pulled myself together and walked outdoors and started to go to pray in the empty church and meditate on the Rising of Christ tomorrow. Along the road as I walked, thinking about the mysteries of Easter, veils!— [*She makes a long shuddering word out of "veils."*] — seemed to drop off my eyes! Light, oh, light! I never have seen such brilliance! It *PRICKED* my eyeballs like *NEEDLES!*

VAL: —Light?

VEE: Yes, yes, light. YOU know, you know we live in light and shadow, that's, that's what we *live* in, a world of—*light* and—*shadow.* . . .

VAL: Yes. In light and shadow. [*He nods with complete understanding and agreement. They are like two children who have found life's meaning, simply and quietly, along a country road.*]

VEE: A world of light and shadow is what we live in, and—it's—confusing. . . .

[*A man is peering in at store window.*]

VAL: Yeah, they—*do* get—*mixed.* . . .

VEE: Well, and then— [*Hesitates to recapture her vision.*] —I heard this clap of thunder! Sky! —Split open! —And there in the split-open sky, I saw, I tell you, I *saw* the TWO HUGE BLAZING EYES OF JESUS CHRIST RISEN! —Not crucified but Risen! I mean Crucified and *then* RISEN! —The blazing eyes of Christ Risen! And then a great— [*Raises both arms and makes a great sweeping motion to describe an apocalyptic disturbance of the atmosphere.*] —His hand! —*Invisible!* —I didn't *see* his hand! —But it *touched* me—here! [*She seizes Val's hand and presses it to her great heaving bosom.*]

TALBOTT [*appearing right in confectionery, furiously*]: VEE!

[*She starts up, throwing the compress from her eyes. Utters a sharp gasp and staggers backward with terror and blasted ecstasy and dismay and belief, all confused in her look.*]

VEE: You!

TALBOTT: VEE!

VEE: *You!*

TALBOTT [*advancing*]: VEE!

VEE [*making two syllables of the word "eyes"*]: —The Ey—es! [*She collapses, forward, falls to her knees, her arms thrown about*

Val. He seizes her to lift her. Two or three men are peering in at the store window]

TALBOTT [*pushing Val away*]: Let go of her, don't put your hands on my wife! [*He seizes her roughly and hauls her to the door. Val moves up to help Vee.*] Don't move. [*At door, to Val:*] I'm coming back.

VAL: I'm not goin' nowhere.

TALBOTT [*to Dog, as he goes off left with Vee*]: Dog, go in there with that boy.

VOICE [*outside*]: Sheriff caught him messin' with his wife.

[*Repeat: Another voice at a distance. "Dog" Hamma enters and stands silently beside the door while there is a continued murmur of excited voices on the street. The following scene should be underplayed, played almost casually, like the performance of some familiar ritual.*]

VAL: What do you want?

[*Dog says nothing but removes from his pocket and opens a spring-blade knife and moves to downstage right. Pee Wee enters. Through the open door—voices.*]

VOICES [*outside*]: —Son of a low-down bitch foolin' with—
—That's right, ought to be—
—Cut the son of a—

VAL: What do you—?

[*Pee Wee closes the door and silently stands beside it, opening a spring-blade knife, Val looks from one to the other.*]

—It's six o'clock. Store's closed.

[*Men chuckle like dry leaves rattling. Val crosses toward the door; is confronted by Talbott; stops short.*]

TALBOTT: Boy, I said stay here.

VAL: I'm not—goin' nowhere. . . .

TALBOTT: Stand back under that light.

VAL: Which light?

TALBOTT: That light. [*Points. Val goes behind counter.*] I want to look at you while I run through some photos of men wanted.

VAL: I'm not wanted.

TALBOTT: A good-looking boy like you is always wanted.

[*Men chuckle, Val stands in hot light under green-shaded bulb, Talbott shuffles through photos he has removed from his pocket.*]

—How tall are you, boy?

VAL: Never measured.

TALBOTT: How much do you weigh?

VAL: Never weighed.

TALBOTT: Got any scars or marks of identification on your face or body?

VAL: No, sir.

TALBOTT: Open your shirt.

VAL: What for? [*He doesn't.*]

TALBOTT: Open his shirt for him, Dog.

[*Dog steps quickly forward and rips shirt open to waist. Val starts forward; men point knives; he draws back.*]

That's right, stay there, boy. What did you do before?

[*Pee Wee sits on stairs.*]

VAL: Before—what?

TALBOTT: Before you come here?

VAL: —Traveled and—played. . . .

TALBOTT: Played?

DOG [*advancing to center*]: What?

PEE WEE: With wimmen?

[DOG *laughs.*]

VAL: No. Played guitar—and sang. . . . [*Val touches guitar on counter.*]

TALBOTT: Let me see that guitar.

VAL: Look at it. But don't touch it. I don't let nobody but musicians touch it.

[*Men come close.*]

DOG: What're you smiling for, boy?

PEE WEE: He ain't smiling, his mouth's just twitching like a dead chicken's foot.

[*They laugh.*]

TALBOTT: What is all that writing on the guitar?

VAL: —Names. . . .

TALBOTT: What of?

VAL: Autographs of musicians dead and living.

[*Men read aloud the names printed on the guitar: Bessie Smith, Leadbelly, Woody Guthrie, Jelly Roll Morton, etc. They bend close to it, keeping the open knife blades pointed at Val's body; Dog touches neck of the guitar, draws it toward him. Val suddenly springs, with catlike agility, onto the counter. He runs along it, kicking at their hands as they catch at his legs. The Nurse runs down to the landing.*]

NURSE: *What's going on?*

TALBOTT [*at the same time*]: *Stop that!*

[*Jabe calls hoarsely above.*]

NURSE [*excitedly, all in one breath, as Jabe calls*]: Where's Mrs. Torrance? I got a very sick man up there and his wife's disappeared. [*Jabe calls out again.*] I been on a whole lot of cases but never seen one where a wife showed no concern for a— [*Jabe cries out again. Her voice fades out as she returns above.*]

TALBOTT [*overlapping Nurse's speech*]: Dog! Pee Wee! You all stand back from that counter. Dog, why don't you an' Pee Wee go up an' see Jabe. Leave me straighten this boy out, go on, go on up.

PEE WEE: C'mon, Dawg. . . .

[*They go up. Val remains panting on counter.*]

TALBOTT [*sits in shoe chair at right window. In his manner there is a curious, half-abashed gentleness, when alone with the boy, as if he recognized the purity in him and was, truly, for the moment, ashamed of the sadism implicit in the occurrence*]: Awright, boy. Git on down off th' counter, I ain't gonna touch y'r guitar.

[*Val jumps off counter.*]

But I'm gonna tell you something. They's a certain county I know of which has a big sign at the county line that says, "Nigger, don't let the sun go down on you in this county." That's all it says, it don't threaten nothing, it just says, "Nigger, don't let the sun go down on you in this county!" [*Chuckles hoarsely. Rises and takes a step toward Val.*] Well, son! You ain't a nigger and this is not that county, but, son, I want you to just imagine that you seen a sign that said to you: "Boy, don't let the sun rise on you in this county." I said "rise," not "go down" because it's too close to sunset for you to git packed an' move on before that. But I think if you value that instrument in your hands as much as you seem to, you'll simplify my job by not allowing the sun tomorrow to rise on you in this county. 'S that understood, now, boy?

[*Val stares at him, expressionless, panting.*]

[*Crossing to door.*] I *hope* so. I don't like *violence.* [*He looks back and nods at Val from the door. Then goes outside in the fiery afterglow of the sunset. Dogs bark in the distance. Music fades in: "Dog Howl Blues"—minor—guitar. Pause in which Val remains motionless, cradling guitar in his arms. Then Val's faraway, troubled look is resolved in a slight, abrupt nod of his head. He sweeps back the alcove curtain and enters the alcove and closes the curtain behind him. Lights dim down to indicate a division of scenes.*]

SCENE THREE

*Half an hour later. The lighting is less realistic than in the previous
scenes of the play. The interior of the store is so dim that only the
vertical lines of the pillars and such selected items as the palm tree
on the stair landing and the ghostly paper vineyard of the confectionery are plainly visible. The view through the great front window has virtually become the background of the action: A singing
wind sweeps clouds before the moon so that the witchlike country
brightens and dims and brightens again. The marshal's hounds are
restless: their baying is heard now and then. A lamp outside the
door sometimes catches a figure that moves past with mysterious
urgency, calling out softly and raising an arm to beckon, like a
shade in the under kingdom.*

*At rise, or when the stage is lighted again, it is empty but foot-
steps are descending the stairs as Dolly and Beulah rush into the
store and call out, in soft shouts:*

DOLLY: Dawg?

BEULAH: Pee Wee?

EVA TEMPLE [*appearing on landing and calling down softly
in the superior tone of a privileged attendant in a sick-chamber*]:
Please don't shout! —Mr. Binnings and Mr. Hamma [*Names of the
two husbands.*] are upstairs sitting with Jabe. . . . [*She continues
her descent. Then Sister Temple appears, sobbing, on landing.*] —
Come down carefully, Sister.

SISTER: Help me, I'm all to pieces. . . .

[*Eva ignores this request and faces the two women.*]

BEULAH: Has the bleedin' quit yit?

EVA: The hemorrhage seems to have stopped. Sister, Sister, pull
yourself together, we all have to face these things sometime in life.

DOLLY: Has he sunk into a coma?

EVA: No. Cousin Jabe is conscious. Nurse Porter says his pulse is remarkably strong for a man that lost so much blood. Of course he's had a transfusion.

SISTER: Two of 'em.

EVA [*crossing to Dolly*] : Yais, an' they put him on glucose. His strength came back like magic.

BEULAH: She up there?

EVA: *Who?*

BEULAH: Lady!

EVA: No! When last reported she had just stepped into the Glorious Hill Beauty Parlor.

BEULAH: You don't mean it.

EVA: Ask Sister!

SISTER: She's planning to go ahead with—!

EVA: —The gala opening of the confectionery. Switch on the lights in there, Sister.

[*Sister crosses and switches on lights and moves off right. The decorated confectionery is lighted, Dolly and Beulah exclaim in awed voices.*]

—Of course it's not normal behavior; it's downright lunacy, but still that's no excuse for it! And when she called up at five, about one hour ago, it wasn't to ask about Jabe, oh, no, she didn't mention his name. She asked if Ruby Lightfoot had delivered a case of Seagram's. Yais, she just shouted that question and hung up the phone, before I could— [*She crosses and goes off.*]

BEULAH [*going into confectionery*]: *Oh, I understand, now! Now I see what she's up to!* Electric moon, cutout silver-paper stars and artificial vines? Why, it's her father's wine garden on Moon Lake she's turned this room into!

DOLLY [*suddenly as she sits in shoe chair*]: *Here she comes, here she comes!*

[*The Temple Sisters retreat from view in confectionery as Lady enters the store. She wears a hooded rain-cape and carries a large paper shopping bag and paper carton box.*]

LADY: Go on, ladies, don't stop, my ears are burning!

BEULAH [*coming to upstage right-center*]: —Lady, oh, Lady, Lady. . . .

LADY: Why d'you speak my name in that pitiful voice? Hanh? [*Throws back hood of cape, her eyes blazing, and places bag and box on counter.*] Val? Val! Where is that boy that works here?

[*Dolly shakes her head.*]

I guess he's havin' a T-bone steak with French fries and cole-slaw fo' ninety-five cents at the Blue Bird. . . .

[*Sounds in confectionery.*]

Who's in the confectionery, is that you, Val?

[*Temple Sisters emerge and stalk past her.*]

Going, girls?

[*They go out of store.*]

Yes, gone! [*She laughs and throws off rain-cape, onto counter, revealing a low-cut gown, triple strand of pearls and a purple satin-ribboned corsage.*]

BEULAH [*sadly*]: How long have I known you, Lady?

LADY [*going behind counter, unpacks paper hats and whistles*]: A long time, Beulah. I think you remember when my people come here on a banana boat from Palermo, Sicily, by way of Caracas, Venezuela, yes, with a grind-organ and a monkey my papa had bought in Venezuela. I was not much bigger than the monkey, ha ha! You remember the monkey? The man that sold Papa the monkey said it was a very young monkey, but he was a liar, it was a very old monkey, it was on its last legs, ha ha ha! But it was a well-dressed monkey. [*Coming to right of counter.*] It had a green velvet suit and a little red cap that it tipped and a tambourine that it passed around for money, ha ha ha. . . . The grind-organ played and the monkey danced in the sun, ha ha! —"*O Sole Mio, Da Da Da daaa. . .!*" [*She sits in chair at counter.*] —One day, the monkey danced too much in the sun and it was a very old monkey and it dropped dead. . . . My Papa, he turned to the people, he made them a bow and he said, "The show is over, the monkey is dead." Ha ha!

[*Slight pause. Then Dolly pipes up venomously:*]

DOLLY: Ain't it wonderful Lady can be so brave?

BEULAH: Yaiss, wonderful! Hanh. . . .

LADY: For me the show is not over, the monkey is not dead yet! [*Then suddenly:*] Val, is that you, Val?

[*Someone has entered the confectionery door, out of sight, and the draught of air has set the wind-chimes tinkling wildly. Lady rushes forward but stops short as Carol appears. She wears a trench coat and a white sailor's cap with a turned-down brim, inscribed with the name of a vessel and a date, past or future, memory or anticipation.*]

DOLLY: Well, here's your first customer, Lady.

LADY [*going behind counter*]: —Carol, that room ain't open.

CAROL: There's a big sign outside that says "Open Tonite!"

LADY: It ain't open to you.

CAROL: I have to stay here a while. They stopped my car, you see, I don't have a license; my license has been revoked and I have to find someone to drive me across the river.

LADY: You can call a taxi.

CAROL: I heard that the boy that works for you is leaving tonight and I—

LADY: *Who said he's leaving?*

CAROL [*crossing to counter*]: Sheriff Talbott. The county marshal suggested I get him to drive me over the river since he'd be crossing it too.

LADY: You got some mighty wrong information!

CAROL: Where is he? I don't see him?

LADY: Why d'you keep coming back here bothering that boy? He's not interested in you! Why would he be leaving here tonight? [*Door opens off as she comes from behind counter.*] Val, is that you, Val?

[*Conjure Man enters through confectionery, mumbling rapidly, holding out something. Beulah and Dolly take flight out the door with cries of revulsion.*]

No conjure stuff, go away!

[*He starts to withdraw.*]

CAROL [*crossing to upstage right-center*]: Uncle! The Choctaw cry! I'll give you a dollar for it.

[*Lady turns away with a gasp, with a gesture of refusal. The Negro nods, then throws back his turkey neck and utters a series of sharp barking sounds that rise to a sustained cry of great intensity and wildness. The cry produces a violent reaction in the building. Beulah and Dolly run out of the store. Lady does not move but she catches her breath. Dog and Pee Wee run down the stairs with ad libs and hustle the Negro out of the store, ignoring Lady, as their wives call: "Pee Wee!" and "Dawg!" outside on the walk. Val sweeps back the alcove curtain and appears as if the cry were his cue. Above, in the sick room, hoarse, outraged shouts that subside with exhaustion. Carol crosses downstage and speaks to the audience and to herself.*]

CAROL: Something is still wild in the country! This country used to be wild, the men and women were wild and there was a wild sort of sweetness in their hearts, for each other, but now it's sick with neon, it's broken out sick, with neon, like most other places. . . . I'll wait outside in my car. It's the fastest thing on wheels in Two River County! [*She goes out of the store right. Lady stares at Val with great asking eyes, a hand to her throat.*]

LADY [*with false boldness*]: Well, ain't you going with her?

VAL: I'm going with no one I didn't come here with. And I come here with no one.

LADY: Then get into your white jacket. I need your services in that room there tonight.

[*Val regards her steadily for several beats.*]

[*Clapping her hands together twice.*] Move, move, stop goofing! The Delta Brilliant lets out in half'n hour and they'll be driving up here. You got to shave ice for the setups!

VAL [*as if he thought she'd gone crazy*]: "Shave ice for the setups"? [*He moves up to counter.*]

LADY: Yes, an' call Ruby Lightfoot, tell her I need me a dozen more half-pints of Seagram's. They all call for Seven-and-Sevens. You know how t' sell bottle goods under a counter? It's OK. We're gonna git paid for protection. [*Gasps, touching her diaphragm.*] But one thing you gotta watch out for is sellin' to minors. Don't serve liquor to minors. Ask for his driver's license if they's any doubt. Anybody born earlier than—let's see, twenty-one from— oh, I'll figure it later. Hey! Move! Move! Stop goofing!

VAL [*placing guitar on counter*]: —You're the one that's goofing, not me, Lady.

LADY: Move, I said, *move!*

VAL: What kick are you on, are you on a benny kick, Lady? 'Ve you washed down a couple of bennies with a pot of black coffee t' make you come on strong for th' three o'clock show? [*His mockery is gentle, almost tender, but he has already made a departure; he is back in the all-night bars with the B-girls and raffish entertainers. He stands at counter as she rushes about. As she crosses between the two rooms, he reaches out to catch hold of her bare arm and he pulls her to him and grips her arms.*]

LADY: Hey!

VAL: Will you quit thrashin' around like a hooked catfish?

LADY: Go git in y'r white jacket an'—

VAL: Sit down. I want to talk to you.

LADY: I don't have time.

VAL: I got to reason with you.

LADY: It's not possible to.

VAL: You can't open a night-place here this night.

LADY: You bet your sweet life I'm *going* to!

VAL: Not *me*, not *my* sweet life!

LADY: I'm betting *my* life on it! Sweet or *not* sweet, I'm—

VAL: Yours is yours, mine *is* mine. . . . [*He releases her with a sad shrug.*]

LADY: You don't get the point, huh? There's a man up there that set fire to my father's wine garden and I lost my life in it, yeah, I lost my life in it, *three* lives was lost in it, two *born* lives and one— not. . . . I was made to commit a *murder* by him up there! [*Has frozen momentarily.*] —I want that man to see the wine garden come open again when he's dying! I want him to hear it coming open again here tonight! While he's dying. It's necessary, no power on earth can stop it. Hell, I don't even want it, it's just necessary, it's just something's got to be done to square things away, to, to, to—be *not defeated! You get me? Just to be not defeated!* Ah, oh, I won't be defeated, not again, in my life! [*Embraces him.*] Thank you for staying here with me! —God bless you for it. . . . Now please go and get in your white jacket . . .

[*Val looks at her as if he were trying to decide between a natural sensibility of heart and what his life's taught him since he left Witches Bayou. Then he sighs again, with the same slight, sad shrug, and crosses into alcove to put on a jacket and remove from under his cot a canvas-wrapped package of his belongings. Lady takes paper hats and carnival stuff from counter, crosses into confectionery and puts them on the tables, then starts back but stops short as she sees Val come out of alcove with his snakeskin jacket and luggage.*]

LADY: That's not your white jacket, that's that snakeskin jacket you had on when you come here.

VAL: I come and I go in this jacket.

LADY: *Go,* did you say?

VAL: Yes, ma'am, I did, I said go. All that stays to be settled is a little matter of wages.

[*The dreaded thing's happened to her. This is what they call "the moment of truth" in the bull ring, when the matador goes in over the horns of the bull to plant the mortal sword-thrust.*]

LADY: —So you're—cutting out, are you?

VAL: My gear's all packed. I'm catchin' the southbound bus.

LADY: Uh-huh, in a pig's eye. You're not conning me, mister. She's waiting for you outside in her high-powered car and you're—

[*Sudden footsteps on stairs. They break apart, Val puts suitcase down, drawing back into shadow, as Nurse Porter appears on the stair landing.*]

NURSE: Mrs. Torrance, are you down there?

LADY [*crossing to foot of stairs*]: Yeah. I'm here. I'm back.

NURSE: Can I talk to you up here about Mr. Torrance?

LADY [*shouting to Nurse*]: I'll be up in a minute.

[*Door closes above. Lady turns to Val.*] Okay, now, mister. You're scared about something, ain't you?

VAL: I been threatened with violence if I stay here.

LADY: I got paid for protection in this county, plenty paid for it, and it covers you too.

VAL: No, ma'am. My time is up here.

LADY: Y' say that like you'd served a sentence in jail.

VAL: I got in deeper than I meant to, Lady.

LADY: Yeah, and how about me?

VAL [*going to her*]: I would of cut out before you got back to the store, but I wanted to tell you something I never told no one before. [*Places hand on her shoulder.*] I feel a true love for you, Lady! [*He kisses her.*] I'll wait for you out of this county, just name the time and the . . .

LADY [*moving back*]: Oh, don't talk about love, not to me. It's easy to say "Love, Love!" with fast and free transportation waiting right out the door for you!

VAL: D'you remember some things I told you about me the night we met here?

LADY [*crossing to right-center*]: Yeah, many things. Yeah, temperature of a dog. And some bird, oh, yeah, without legs so it had to sleep on the wind!

VAL [*through her speech*]: Naw, not that; not that.

LADY: And how you could burn down a woman? I said "Bull!" I take that back. You can! You can burn down a woman and stamp on her ashes to make sure the fire is put out!

VAL: I mean what I said about gettin' away from . . .

LADY: How long've you held this first steady job in your life?

VAL: Too long, too long!

LADY: Four months and five days, mister. All right! How much pay have you took?

VAL: I told you to keep out all but—

LADY: Y'r living expenses. I can give you the figures to a dime.

115

Eighty-five bucks, no, ninety? Chicken feed, mister! Y'know how much you got coming? IF you get it? I don't need paper to figure, I got it all in my head. You got five hundred and eighty-six bucks coming to you, not, not chicken feed, that. But, mister. [*Gasps for breath.*] —If you try to walk out on me, now, tonight, without notice! —You're going to get just nothing! A great big zero. . . .

[*Somebody hollers at door off right: "Hey! You open?" She rushes toward it shouting, "CLOSED! CLOSED! GO AWAY!" —Val crosses to the cashbox. She turns back toward him, gasps.*]

Now you watch your next move and I'll watch mine. You open that cashbox and I swear I'll throw open that door and holler, clerk's robbing the store!

VAL: —Lady?

LADY [*fiercely*]: Hanh?

VAL: —Nothing, you've—

LADY: —Hanh?

VAL: Blown your stack. I will go without pay.

LADY [*coming to center*]: Then you ain't understood me! With or without pay, you're staying!

VAL: I've got my gear. [*Picks up suitcase. She rushes to seize his guitar.*]

LADY: Then I'll go up and git mine! And take this with me, just t'make sure you wait till I'm— [*She moves back. He puts suitcase down.*]

VAL [*advancing toward her*]: Lady, what're you—?

LADY [*entreating with guitar raised*]: Don't—!

VAL: —Doing with—

LADY: —*Don't!*

VAL: —my guitar!

LADY: *Holding it for security while I—*

VAL: Lady, you been a lunatic since this morning!

LADY: Longer, longer than morning! I'm going to keep hold of your "life companion" while I pack! I am! I am goin' to pack an' go, if you go, where you go!

[*He makes a move toward her. She crosses below and around to counter.*]

You didn't think so, you actually didn't think so? What was I going to do, in your opinion? What, in your opinion, would I be doing? Stay on here in a store full of bottles and boxes while you go far, while you go fast and far, without me having your—forwarding address!—even?

VAL: I'll—give you a forwarding address. . . .

LADY: Thanks, oh, thanks! Would I take your forwarding address back of that curtain? "Oh, dear forwarding address, hold me, kiss me, be faithful!" [*Utters grotesque, stifled cry; presses fist to mouth.*]

[*He advances cautiously, hand stretched toward the guitar. She retreats above to upstage right-center, biting lip, eyes flaring. Jabe knocks above.*]

Stay back! You want me to smash it!

VAL [*downstage center*]: He's—knocking for you. . . .

LADY: I know! Death's knocking for me! Don't you think I hear him, knock, knock, knock? It sounds like what it is! Bones knocking bones. . . . Ask me how it felt to be coupled with death up there, and I can tell you. My skin crawled when he touched me. But I endured it. I guess my heart knew that somebody must be coming to take me out of this hell! You did. You came. Now look at me! I'm alive once more! [*Convulsive sobbing controlled: continues more calmly and harshly.*] —I won't wither in dark! Got that through your skull? Now. Listen! Everything in this rotten store is yours, not just your pay, but everything Death's scraped together down here!—but Death has got to die before we can go. . . . You got that memorized, now?—Then get into your white jacket! —*Tonight is the gala opening*— [*Rushes through confectionery.*] —*of the confectionery*— [*Val runs and seizes her arm holding guitar. She breaks violently free.*] *Smash me against a rock and I'll smash your guitar! I will, if you*—

[*Rapid footsteps on stairs.*]

Oh, Miss Porter!

[*She motions Val back. He retreats into alcove. Lady puts guitar down beside juke box. Miss Porter is descending the stairs.*]

NURSE [*descending watchfully*]: You been out a long time.

LADY [*moving upstage right-center*]: Yeah, well, I had lots of— [*Her voice expires breathlessly. She stares fiercely, blindly, into the other's hard face.*]

NURSE: —Of what?

LADY: Things to—things to—take care of. . . . [*Draws a deep, shuddering breath, clenched fist to her bosom.*]

NURSE: Didn't I hear you shouting to someone just now?

LADY: —Uh-huh. Some drunk tourist made a fuss because I wouldn't sell him no—liquor. . . .

NURSE [*crossing to the door*]: Oh. Mr. Torrance is sleeping under medication.

LADY: That's good. [*She sits in shoe-fitting chair.*]

NURSE: I gave him a hypo at five.

LADY: —Don't all that morphine weaken the heart, Miss Porter?

NURSE: Gradually, yes.

LADY: How long does it usually take for them to let go?

NURSE: It varies according to the age of the patient and the condition his heart's in. Why?

LADY: Miss Porter, don't people sort of help them let go?

NURSE: How do you mean, Mrs. Torrance?

LADY: Shorten their suffering for them?

NURSE: Oh, I see what you mean. [*Snaps her purse shut.*] —I see what you mean, Mrs. Torrance. But killing is killing, regardless of circumstances.

LADY: Nobody said killing.

NURSE: You said "shorten their suffering."

LADY: Yes, like merciful people shorten an animal's suffering when he's. . . .

NURSE: A human being is not the same as an animal, Mrs. Torrance. And I don't hold with what they call—

LADY [*overlapping*]: *Don't give me a sermon*, Miss Porter. I just wanted to know if—

NURSE [*overlapping*]: I'm not giving a sermon. I just answered your question. If you want to get somebody to shorten your husband's life—

LADY [*jumping up; overlapping*]: Why, how dare you say that I—

NURSE: I'll be back at ten-thirty.

LADY: Don't!

NURSE: What?

LADY [*crossing behind counter*]: Don't come back at ten-thirty, don't come back.

NURSE: I'm always discharged by the doctors on my cases.

LADY: This time you're being discharged by the patient's wife.

NURSE: That's something we'll have to discuss with Dr. Buchanan.

LADY: I'll call him myself about it. I don't like you. I don't think you belong in the nursing profession, you have cold eyes; I think you like to watch pain!

NURSE: I know why you don't like my eyes. [*Snaps purse shut.*] You don't like my eyes because you know they see clear.

LADY: Why are you staring at *me?*

NURSE: I'm not staring at you, I'm staring at the curtain. There's something burning in there, smoke's coming out! [*Starts toward alcove.*] Oh.

LADY: Oh, no, you don't. [*Seizes her arm.*]

NURSE [*pushes her roughly aside and crosses to the curtain. Val rises from cot, opens the curtain and faces her coolly*]: Oh, excuse me! [*She turns to Lady.*] —The moment I looked at you when I was called on this case last Friday morning I knew that you were pregnant.

[*Lady gasps.*]

I also knew the moment I looked at your husband it wasn't by him. [*She stalks to the door, Lady suddenly cries out:*]

LADY: Thank you for telling me what I hoped for is true.

NURSE: You don't seem to have any shame.

LADY [*exalted*]: No. I don't have shame. I have—great—joy!

NURSE [*venomously*]: Then why don't you get the calliope and the clown to make the announcement?

LADY: You do it for me, save me the money! Make the announcement, all over!

[*Nurse goes out. Val crosses swiftly to the door and locks it. Then he advances toward her, saying:*]

VAL: Is it true what she said?

[*Lady moves as if stunned to the counter; the stunned look gradually turns to a look of wonder. On the counter is a heap of silver and gold paper hats and trumpets for the gala opening of the confectionery.*]

VAL [*in a hoarse whisper*]: Is it true or not true, what that woman told you?

LADY: You sound like a scared little boy.

VAL: She's gone out to tell. [*Pause.*]

LADY: You gotta go now—it's dangerous for you to stay

here. . . . Take your pay out of the cashbox, you can go. Go, go, take the keys to my car, cross the river into some other county. You've done what you came here to do. . . .

VAL: —It's true then, it's—?

LADY [*sitting in chair of counter*]: True as God's word! I have life in my body, this dead tree, my body, has burst in flower! You've given me life, you can go!

[*He crouches down gravely opposite her, gently takes hold of her knotted fingers and draws them to his lips, breathing on them as if to warm them. She sits bolt upright, tense, blind as a clairvoyant.*]

VAL: —Why didn't you tell me before?

LADY: —When a woman's been childless as long as I've been childless, it's hard to believe that you're still able to bear! —We used to have a little fig tree between the house and the orchard. It never bore any fruit, they said it was barren. Time went by it, spring after useless spring, and it almost started to—die. . . . Then one day I discovered a small green fig on the tree they said wouldn't bear! [*She is clasping a gilt paper horn.*] I ran through the orchard. I ran through the wine garden shouting, "Oh, Father, it's going to bear, the fig tree is going to bear!"—It seemed such a wonderful thing, after those ten barren springs, for the little fig tree to bear, it called for a celebration—I ran to a closet, I opened a box that we kept Christmas ornaments in! —I took them out, glass bells, glass birds, tinsel, icicles, stars. . . . And I hung the little tree with them, I decorated the fig tree with glass bells and glass birds, and silver icicles and stars, because it won the battle and it would bear! [*Rises, ecstatic.*] Unpack the box! Unpack the box with the Christmas ornaments in it, put them on me, glass bells and glass birds and stars and tinsel and snow! [*In a sort of delirium she thrusts the conical gilt paper hat on her head and runs to the foot of the stairs with the paper horn. She blows the horn over and over, grotesquely mounting the stairs, as Val tries to stop her. She breaks away from him and runs up to the landing, blowing the paper horn and crying out:*] I've won, I've won, Mr. Death, I'm going to bear! [*Then suddenly she falters, catches her breath in a shocked gasp and awkwardly retreats to the stairs. Then turns screaming and runs back down them, her cries dying out as she arrives at the floor level. She retreats haltingly as a blind person, a hand stretched out to Val, as slow, clumping footsteps and hoarse breathing are heard on the stairs. She moans:*] —Oh, God, oh— God. . . . [*Jabe appears on the landing, by the artificial palm tree in its dully lustrous green jardiniere, a stained purple robe hangs loosely about his wasted yellowed frame. He is Death's self, and malignancy, as he peers, crouching, down into the store's dimness to discover his quarry.*]

JABE: Buzzards! Buzzards! [*Clutching the trunk of the false palm tree, he raises the other hand holding a revolver and fires down into the store, Lady screams and rushes to cover Val's motionless figure with hers, Jabe scrambles down a few steps and fires again and the bullet strikes her, expelling her breath in a great "Hah!" He fires again; the great "Hah!" is repeated. She turns to face him, still covering Val with her body, her face with all the passions and secrets of life and death in it now, her fierce eyes blazing, knowing, defying and accepting. But the revolver is empty; it clicks impotently and Jabe hurls it toward them; he descends and passes them, shouting out hoarsely:*] I'll have you burned! I burned her father and I'll have you burned! [*He opens the door and rushes out onto the road, shouting hoarsely:*] The clerk is robbing the store, he shot my wife, the clerk is robbing the store, he killed my wife!

VAL: —Did it—?

LADY: —Yes! —it did. . . .

[*A curious, almost formal, dignity appears in them both. She turns to him with the sort of smile that people offer in apology for an awkward speech, and he looks back at her gravely, raising one hand as if to stay her. But she shakes her head slightly and points to the ghostly radiance of her make-believe orchard and she begins to move a little unsteadily toward it. Music. Lady enters the confectionery and looks about it as people look for the last time at a loved place they are deserting.*]

The show is over. The monkey is dead . . .

[*Music rises to cover whatever sound Death makes in the confectionery. It halts abruptly. Figures appear through the great front window of the store, pocket-lamps stare through the glass and someone begins to force the front door open. Val cries out.*]

VAL: Which way!

[*He turns and runs through the dim radiance of the confectionery, out of our sight. Something slams. Something cracks open. Men are in the store and the dark is full of hoarse, shouting voices.*]

VOICES OF MEN [*shouting*]: —Keep to the walls! He's armed!
—Upstairs, Dog!
—Jack, the confectionery!

[*Wild cry back of store.*]

—Got him. GOT HIM!
—They got him!
—Rope, git rope!
—Git rope from th' hardware section!
—I got something better than rope!
—What've you got?

—What's that, what's he got?
—A BLOWTORCH!
—Christ. . . .

[*A momentary hush.*]

—Come on, what in hell are we waiting for?
—Hold on a minute, I wanta see if it works!
—Wait, wait!
—LOOK here!

[*A jet of blue flame stabs the dark. It flickers on Carol's figure in the confectionery. The men cry out together in hoarse passion crouching toward the fierce blue jet of fire, their faces lit by it like the faces of demons.*]

—Christ!
—It works!

[*They rush out. Confused shouting behind. Motors start. Fade quickly. There is almost silence, a dog bays in the distance. Then— the Conjure Man appears with a bundle of garments which he examines, dropping them all except the snakeskin jacket, which he holds up with a toothless mumble of excitement.*]

CAROL [*quietly, gently*]: What have you got there, Uncle? Come here and let me see. [*He crosses to her.*] Oh yes, his snakeskin jacket. I'll give you a gold ring for it. [*She slowly twists ring off her finger. Somewhere there is a cry of anguish. She listens attentively till it fades out, then nods with understanding.*] —Wild things leave skins behind them, they leave clean skins and teeth and white bones behind them, and these are tokens passed from one to another, so that the fugitive kind can always follow their kind. . . .

[*The cry is repeated more terribly than before. It expires again. She draws the jacket about her as if she were cold, nods to the old Negro, handing him the ring. Then she crosses toward the door, pausing halfway as Sheriff Talbott enters with his pocket-lamp.*]

TALBOTT: Don't no one move, don't move!

[*She crosses directly past him as if she no longer saw him, and out the door. He shouts furiously:*]

Stay here!

[*Her laughter rings outside. He follows the girl, shouting:*]

Stop! Stop!

[*Silence. The Negro looks up with a secret smile as the curtain falls slowly.*]

INTRODUCTION TO
SUDDENLY LAST SUMMER

Paul Bowles moved to Tangier in 1947. A respected composer, he had written the music for the original production of *The Glass Menagerie* in 1945, as well as incidental music for the Broadway productions of *A Streetcar Named Desire* in 1947 and *Summer and Smoke* in 1948. Once ensconced in Morocco he became an admired writer and translator of fiction. But more than anyone, he opened North Africa as an enticing and available garden of delights for the aesthetic homosexual community of his day. If you strip it down to the basics, he wasn't in Tangier for the hummus. Tennessee Williams often visited him. Cabeza de Lobo, in *Suddenly Last Summer,* is a fictionalized version of the Moroccan seaside town Asilah, where Bowles had a house. It is in Cabeza de Lobo that the poet Sebastian Venable meets his grisly end. A generous description of Sebastian's final journey might be "the quest of a highly civilized man for an anti-civilized truth." Which, as it happens, was Norman Mailer's assessment of Paul Bowles's life. I don't think Bowles was a precise model for Sebastian, but surely he and the aesthetes who followed him to Morocco are somewhere in the stew.

Ah, Sebastian Venable. What a wonderful name. One of the most despicable characters Williams ever created, surely. One thinks of him *as* a character; it comes as a shock to remember he never actually appears in the play. But he comes blazingly alive in the monologues of his worshipping mother, Violet, and his distraught cousin, Catharine. Jerry Tallmer, the critic of the *Village Voice* when the play was first produced, called *Suddenly Last Summer*, in what was an unusually candid review for its day, "a wild, bold acknowledgment of homosexuality and a searing attempt to exorcise it and become 'healthy.'" Williams had very publicly entered psychoanalysis shortly before writing the play. In those days, many psychoanalysts believed that homosexuality was at best a dangerous neurosis, and none more so than Lawrence Kubie, Williams's charismatic doctor. Kubie treated many prominent, albeit closeted, gay men in the arts; in essence, if not in actuality, he attempted to *cure* them, and according to Williams, suggested that he give up both gay sex and writing. A double cure, I suppose. Williams did neither. He wrote *Suddenly Last Summer* in the mornings and went to sessions with the good doctor in the afternoons. His attitude to what he was writing, and then what he was saying, must have been ambiguous and conflicted. Williams seems to mock Sebastian and pour contempt on him (which would have pleased Kubie), and yet might he not have admired him as well? What if Violet's laudatory description of her son possessed some kind of truth?

A minor poet travels the world accompanied by a woman. He is selfishly dedicated to his art and will exploit those around him to stay true to it. But, sadly, his creativity has run dry. He ends up, with his young companion, in a distant tropical hellhole. A partial description of Sebastian, certainly, but equally a description of Nonno in *The Night Of the Iguana*. This play, written only three years after *Suddenly Last Summer*, features a variation of the same character, sexual content aside, but this time Nonno (his real name, Jonathan Coffin—another gem), is as admirable as Sebastian is not. It would seem that there was something Williams could not get out of his system, something he had conflicting and changeable views about. It is often assumed that Williams, in recounting Sebastian's "journey," was writing about homosexuals as both devouring and being devoured, but it seems to me more likely that he was writing about artists in the same terms. Or perhaps, to him, the two were indistinguishable. Williams wasn't baring his soul to Kubie because of contentment; he was plagued with guilt, fear, and insecurity, much of which revolved around both his writing and his sexuality, the latter being a matter of public disgrace and criminality in the fifties. Perhaps it explains Kubie's suggestion to give up both.

Suddenly Last Summer certainly perplexed Dr. Kubie, whose abhorrence of matters gay was tested to the limit by Sebastian's fate. In a letter to Williams, after seeing the play, he confessed to being mystified by "the fantasy of eating and being eaten," which is "pretty cloudy to me." Poor Kubie. He was confused because the artist was confused. But as Williams was an extraordinary artist, the confusion seems not like confusion, but an enormous truth. But what truth?

Williams tried later, with Nonno, to find another, gentler way of projecting an artist's sensibility and destiny. And yet Nonno is at heart as selfish as Sebastian. This time the writer is not condemning him for it; if anything, he is extolling him. Well, to a point. If you neglect the central "n" in the ancient poet's name, Williams is suggesting No–No. And yet, everything we know about Williams tells us that his feeling about creating art was Yes–Yes. It is impossible to pin down what Williams actually felt, because he felt so many things at the same time; not only are his characters filled with contradictions, but the plays are themselves. Even as I write this introduction, trying to analyze one particular play, I find myself spinning in circles.

As for his two doomed poets—both die at the play's conclusion and, together with Val Xavier, the handsome drifter in *Orpheus Descending* who began life as a poet in *Battle Of Angels*, they are the *only* three male characters to expire in the major Williams plays—if selfishness is necessary for Nonno's art, isn't it also for Sebastian's? Nonno, incidentally, ends up writing a beautiful poem, while it is usually assumed that Sebastian's work is pretentious. But who is to say that Sebastian wasn't actually a *good* poet? Williams never lets us hear his work, so he doesn't really commit himself; with Nonno, he goes for it. Nonetheless, Williams seems to be criticizing himself (the homosexual writer) in the first play, as well as looking beadily at friends like Bowles, and then suddenly justifying himself and the Bowles clique in the second. Except the criticism (in *Suddenly)* may have an unspoken admiration, and the admiration (in *Iguana*) may be filtered with criticism. If the observer must argue with himself trying to figure out what on earth the playwright was thinking, so too most probably did the playwright, who had no choice but to write two versions of the same conceit. Dr. Kubie gains the upper hand in *Suddenly Last Summer* and then loses it again in *The Night of the Iguana* (written when Williams was no longer in analysis). Sebastian is, nonetheless, the more potent of the two characters. This, despite the fact that he has died before the play begins.

Of course, Sebastian is only a despicable predator if you believe Catharine's story. The play ends with an unforgettable line—"I think we ought at least to consider the possibility that the girl's story could be true. . . ." Which is, by the way, a recycling of the last line of Williams's original (1955) and final (1973) versions of *Cat On A Hot Tin Roof*—"wouldn't it be funny if that was true?" In both plays an honest observation is being made; Maggie does love Brick, and Catharine's story is accurate.

Or is it? The assumption has always been that Catharine is giving the correct account of what happened to Sebastian on Cabeza de Lobo. Catherine was based, to some degree, on Williams's sister, Rose. Rose had been diagnosed as a paranoid schizophrenic in the late thirties; she was delusional and verbalized sexual fantasies, which was especially shocking behavior for a young woman of her time. She was lobotomized in 1943, a tragedy that haunted Williams forever after. If he has used Rose as a blueprint for Catharine, no matter how craftily disguised, would he not therefore be writing, to some degree, about delusion? Would he not be creating a colorful and unspeakable erotic *fantasy* to match Rose's? Note too that Anne Meacham, who played Catharine in the original production, radiated acute instability; not someone whose word you would necessarily trust. ("She herself was nothing if not high strung," said Jerry Tallmer in Meacham's obituary). The film, on the other hand, had Elizabeth Taylor, an actress so direct that one tended to believe her even if she claimed to be the Queen of Egypt. Such is the power of cinema that when we think of Catharine we think of Taylor, but the original performance was very different, more ambiguous and more disturbing.

Consider also that Williams was basing Catharine not only on Rose, but on himself as well. There is much of Tennessee in *both* Sebastian and Catharine. Williams, the artist, was constantly saying things the world did not want to hear. He spoke— or at least suggested—sexual truths that had always remained hidden. But he fictionalized those truths. What came from his pen was not necessarily literal. So if he instructs us to consider the possibility that Catharine's story is true, should we not also consider the possibility that it isn't? Cutting open Catharine's mind is evil, whether her story is factual or not. Mrs. Venable might be cruel and unjust, just as Catharine is highly sympathetic; but that doesn't necessarily mean the story is accurate. I am not suggesting that it isn't, but rather that we don't know. Williams seems to want us to believe it is true, and yet the power of the play comes from the fact that his subconscious is sending out so many mixed signals. Again, his tumult seems inseparable from his genius.

Williams was haunted by Rose's lobotomy and wracked with guilt for not being able to prevent the surgery. The specter of lobotomy hangs over *Suddenly Last Summer*. The play is driven by two questions: what is the story Violet wants cut out of Catharine's mind, and will the actual cutting take place. The fear of that sadistic operation permeates the jungle garden where the play is set. But, again, is that fear even more personal than one might suspect? Was Williams afraid that somehow his own truths, as well as his fantasies, his gift for elaborate storytelling, would be cut out of *him*? Did he think that somehow he would meet the same fate as his sister? Didn't they, in a sense, have a similar illness, except Rose turned hers into babble and Williams turned his into art? I think Catharine's fear mirrors the writer's. And of course, we never know how the issue is resolved for Catharine, just as Williams had no idea what his own fate would be when he wrote the play. And that outcome would ultimately mirror his worst fears.

As he grew older, his dependence on alcohol and narcotics became legendary and ultimately contributed to his death. Looking at the reports of his last days, and indeed his erratic final writing, it is difficult to believe that the drink and drugs didn't take their toll on his brain as well as his body. It seems to me that some of his brain cells were diminished or reduced. He had begun, creatively, to babble. He had, in essence, self-lobotomized. In the end, he was becoming Rose. The irony is that whereas the author of *Suddenly Last Summer* dreads, deplores and fears the idea of a lobotomy, some part of him also yearns for it.

If Williams's mind was more confused subconsciously when he wrote *Suddenly Last Summer* than it had been or would be when creating his other major work, rarely has his craft been as focused. The play is daring in its construction; it is basically two arias with connective tissue. The second half is one person telling a story. And there is no resolution. And yet it is as tight and taut as anything he ever wrote. There is not a single wasted word. There is none of the wondrous disorder of *Orpheus Descending*. It's as if he had to totally discipline himself in order to give his contradictory mind some dramatic direction. And rarely has the poet in him merged so comfortably with the dramatist. For the poetry in *Suddenly Last Summer* is purely of the theater. Names like Cabeza de Lobo and the Encantadas look dimly exotic in print, but they become utterly evocative and mysterious and even frightening when *spoken*. Catharine's account of the journey becomes transcendent when acted. Words, phrases, sentences assume a rhythm onstage that they do not possess on the page. The play, in its vision of Sebastian, seems to make the idea of poetry look foolish, and yet the writing of it honors poetic imagery in a way that exceeds almost anything else in modern theater. So even its glory resides in the center of a contradiction.

The true genius of *Suddenly Last Summer* is that you believe it; not just Catharine's story, but the whole damn thing. As you read it everything seems to make sense, despite the fact that really it makes no sense whatsoever. A woman entering old age, acting as sexual bait (Violet before her stroke)? A doctor dedicated to removing unfortunate memories from a woman's brain who then injects her with a mysterious truth serum, which might validate those memories? A handsome, dissipated poet who, after twenty-some years of traveling for just such a purpose, still can't figure out how to negotiate a blowjob on his own? One shouldn't really overanalyze *Suddenly Last Summer*. Trying to figure it out can land you in Lion's View. You just have to go with it. It is "intangible and powerful, bringing to mind one of those clouds you have seen in summer, close to the horizon and dark in color and now and then silently pulsing with interior flashes of fire" (Williams, writing about Paul Bowles's novel, *The Sheltering Sky*). Williams, of course, might have been describing his own work, his own dark cloud, which finally because of—not despite—its many contradictions pulsates with fire and has insinuated itself into the collective subconscious of twentieth-century art.

MARTIN SHERMAN

SUDDENLY LAST SUMMER

TO ANNE MEACHAM

Suddenly Last Summer *and the one-act play* Something Unspoken *were presented together under the collective title of* Garden District *at the York Theatre on First Avenue in New York on January 7, 1958, by John C. Wilson and Warner Le Roy. The plays were directed by Herbert Machiz; the stage set was designed by Robert Soule and the costumes by Stanley Simmons. Lighting was by Lee Watson and the incidental music was by Ned Rorem. The cast was as follows:*

MRS. VENABLE	Hortense Alden
DR. CUKROWICZ	Robert Lansing
MISS FOXHILL	Donna Cameron
MRS. HOLLY	Eleanor Phelps
GEORGE HOLLY	Alan Mixon
CATHARINE HOLLY	Anne Meacham
SISTER FELICITY	Nanon-Kiam

Something Unspoken is published in *27 Wagons Full of Cotton and Other Plays.*

SCENE ONE

The set may be as unrealistic as the decor of a dramatic ballet. It represents part of a mansion of Victorian Gothic style in the Garden District of New Orleans on a late afternoon, between late summer and early fall. The interior is blended with a fantastic garden which is more like a tropical jungle, or forest, in the prehistoric age of giant fern-forests when living creatures had flippers turning to limbs and scales to skin. The colors of this jungle-garden are violent, especially since it is steaming with heat after rain. There are massive tree-flowers that suggest organs of a body, torn out, still glistening with undried blood; there are harsh cries and sibilant hissings and thrashing sounds in the garden as if it were inhabited by beasts, serpents and birds, all of savage nature. . . .

The jungle tumult continues a few moments after the curtain rises; then subsides into relative quiet, which is occasionally broken by a new outburst.

A lady enters with the assistance of a silver-knobbed cane. She has light orange or pink hair and wears a lavender lace dress, and over her withered bosom is pinned a starfish of diamonds.

She is followed by a young blond Doctor, all in white, glacially brilliant, very, very good looking, and the old lady's manner and eloquence indicate her undeliberate response to his icy charm.

MRS. VENABLE: Yes, this was Sebastian's garden. The Latin names of the plants were printed on tags attached to them but the print's fading out. Those ones there— [*She draws a deep breath.*] —are the oldest plants on earth, survivors from the age of the giant fern-forests. Of course in this semitropical climate— [*She takes another deep breath.*] —some of the rarest plants, such as the Venus's-flytrap—you know what this is, Doctor? The Venus's-flytrap?

DOCTOR: An insectivorous plant?

MRS. VENABLE: Yes, it feeds on insects. It has to be kept under glass from early fall to late spring and when it went under glass, my son, Sebastian, had to provide it with fruit flies flown in at great expense from a Florida laboratory that used fruit flies for experiments in genetics. Well, I can't do that, Doctor. [*She takes a deep breath.*] I can't, I just can't do it! It's not the expense but the—

DOCTOR: Effort.

MRS. VENABLE: Yes. So goodbye, Venus's-flytrap—like so much else. . . . Whew! . . . [*She draws breath.*] —I don't know why, but—! I already feel I can lean on your shoulder, Doctor—Cu? —Cu?

DOCTOR: Cu-kro-wicz. It's a Polish word that means sugar, so let's make it simple and call me Doctor Sugar. [*He returns her smile.*]

MRS. VENABLE: Well, now, Doctor Sugar, you've seen Sebastian's garden.

[*They are advancing slowly to the patio area.*]

DOCTOR: It's like a well-groomed jungle. . . .

MRS. VENABLE: That's how he meant it to be, nothing was accidental, everything was planned and designed in Sebastian's life and his— [*She dabs her forehead with her handkerchief which she had taken from her reticule.*] —work!

DOCTOR: What was your son's work, Mrs. Venable?—besides this garden?

MRS. VENABLE: As many times as I've had to answer that question! D'you know it still shocks me a little?—to realize that Sebastian Venable the poet is still unknown outside of a small coterie of friends, including his mother.

DOCTOR: Oh.

MRS. VENABLE: You see, strictly speaking, his *life* was his occupation.

DOCTOR: I see.

MRS. VENABLE: No, you *don't* see, yet, but before I'm through, you will. —Sebastian was a poet! That's what I meant when I said his life was his work because the work of a poet is the life of a poet and—vice versa, the life of a poet is the work of a poet, I mean you can't separate them, I mean—well, for instance, a salesman's work is one thing and his life is another—or can be. The same thing's true of—doctor, lawyer, merchant, *thief*! —But a poet's life is his work and his work is his life in a special sense because—oh, I've already talked myself breathless and dizzy. [*The Doctor offers his arm.*] Thank you.

DOCTOR: Mrs. Venable, did your doctor okay this thing?

MRS. VENABLE [*breathless*]: What thing?

DOCTOR: Your meeting this girl that you think is responsible for your son's death?

MRS. VENABLE: I've waited months to face her because I couldn't get to St. Mary's to face her—I've had her brought here to my house. I won't collapse! She'll collapse! I mean her lies will collapse—not my truth—not the truth. . . . *Forward march, Doctor Sugar!*

[*He conducts her slowly to the patio.*]

Ah, we've *made* it, *ha ha*! I didn't know that I was so weak on my pins! Sit down, Doctor. I'm not afraid of using every last ounce and inch of my little, leftover strength in doing just what I'm doing. I'm devoting all that's left of my life, Doctor, to the defense of a dead poet's reputation. Sebastian had no public name as a poet, he didn't want one, he refused to have one. He *dreaded, abhorred*—false values that come from being publicly known, from fame, from personal—exploitation. . . . Oh, he'd say to me: "Violet? Mother? —You're going to outlive me!!"

DOCTOR: What made him think that?

MRS. VENABLE: Poets are always clairvoyant! —And he had rheumatic fever when he was fifteen and it affected a heart-valve and he wouldn't stay off horses and out of water and so forth. . . . "Violet? Mother? You're going to live longer than me, and then, when I'm gone, it will be yours, in your hands, to do whatever you please with!"—Meaning, of course, his future recognition! —That he *did* want, he wanted it after his death when it couldn't disturb him; then he did want to offer his work to the world. All right. Have I made my point, Doctor? Well, here is my son's work, Doctor, here's his life going *on*!

[*She lifts a thin gilt-edged volume from the patio table as if elevating the Host before the altar. Its gold leaf and lettering catch the afternoon sun. It says* Poem of Summer. *Her face suddenly has a different look, the look of a visionary, an exalted* religieuse. *At the same instant a bird sings clearly and purely in the garden and the old lady seems to be almost young for a moment.*]

DOCTOR [*reading the title*]: Poem of Summer?

MRS. VENABLE: *Poem of Summer,* and the date of the summer, there are twenty-five of them, he wrote one poem a year which he printed himself on an eighteenth-century hand press at his—atelier in the—French—Quarter—so no one but he could see it. . . . [*She seems dizzy for a moment.*]

DOCTOR: He wrote one poem a year?

140

MRS. VENABLE: One for each summer that we traveled together. The other nine months of the year were really only a preparation.

DOCTOR: Nine months?

MRS. VENABLE: The length of a pregnancy, yes. . . .

DOCTOR: The poem was hard to deliver?

MRS. VENABLE: Yes, even with me! *Without* me, *impossible,* Doctor! —he wrote no poem last summer.

DOCTOR: He died last summer?

MRS. VENABLE: Without me he died last summer, that was his last summer's poem. [*She staggers; he assists her toward a chair. She catches her breath with difficulty.*] One long-ago summer—now, why am I thinking of this? —my son, Sebastian, said, "Mother?—Listen to this!"—He read me Herman Melville's description of the Encantadas, the Galápagos Islands. Quote—take five and twenty heaps of cinders dumped here and there in an outside city lot. Imagine some of them magnified into mountains, and the vacant lot, the sea. And you'll have a fit idea of the general aspect of the Encantadas, the Enchanted Isles—extinct volcanos, looking much as the world at large might look—after a last conflagration—end quote. He read me that description and said that we had to go there. And so we did go there that summer on a chartered boat, a four-masted schooner, as close as possible to the sort of a boat that Melville must have sailed on. . . . We saw the Encantadas, but on the Encantadas we saw something Melville *hadn't* written about. We saw the great sea turtles crawl up out of the sea for their annual egg-laying. . . . Once a year the female of the sea turtle crawls up out of the equatorial sea onto the blazing sand-beach of a volcanic island to dig a pit in the sand and deposit her eggs there. It's a long and dreadful thing, the depositing of the eggs in the sand pits, and when it's finished the exhausted female turtle crawls back to the sea half dead. She never sees her offspring, but we did. Sebastian knew exactly when the sea turtle eggs would be hatched out and we returned in time for it. . .

DOCTOR: You went back to the—?

MRS. VENABLE: Terrible Encantadas, those heaps of extinct volcanos, in time to witness the hatching of the sea turtles and their desperate flight to the sea! [*There is a sound of harsh bird-cries in the air. She looks up.*] —The narrow beach, the color of caviar, was all in motion! But the sky was in motion, too. . . .

DOCTOR: The sky was in motion, too?

MRS. VENABLE: —Full of flesh-eating birds and the noise of the birds, the horrible savage cries of the—

DOCTOR: Carnivorous birds?

MRS. VENABLE: Over the narrow black beach of the Encantadas as the just-hatched sea turtles scrambled out of the sand pits and started their race to the sea. . . .

DOCTOR: Race to the sea?

MRS. VENABLE: To escape the flesh-eating birds that made the sky almost as black as the beach! [*She gazes up again: we hear the wild, ravenous, harsh cries of the birds. The sound comes in rhythmic waves like a savage chant.*] And the sand all alive, all alive, as the hatched sea-turtles made their dash for the sea, while the birds hovered and swooped to attack and hovered and—swooped to attack! They were diving down on the hatched sea turtles, turning them over to expose their soft undersides, tearing the undersides open and rending and eating their flesh. Sebastian guessed that possibly only a hundredth of one per cent of their number would escape to the sea. . . .

DOCTOR: What was it about this spectacle on the beach that fascinated your son?

MRS. VENABLE: My son was looking for— [*Stops short: continues evasively*—] Let's just say he was interested in sea turtles.

DOCTOR: You started to say that your son was looking for something.

MRS. VENABLE [*defiantly*]: All right, I started to say that my son was looking for God and I stopped myself because I was afraid that if I said he was looking for God, you'd say to yourself, "Oh, a pretentious young crackpot!"—which Sebastian was not. All poets look for God, all good poets do, and they have to look harder for Him than priests do since they don't have the help of such famous guidebooks and well-organized expeditions as priests have with their scriptures and churches. All right! Well, now I've said it, my son was looking for God. I mean for a clear image of Him. He spent that whole blazing equatorial day in the crow's nest of the schooner watching that thing on the beach of the Encantadas till it was too dark to see it, and when he came back down the rigging, he said, Well, now I've seen Him! —and he meant God . . .

DOCTOR: I see.

MRS. VENABLE: For several days after that he had a fever, he was delirious with it. I took command of the ship and we sailed north by east into cooler waters . . .

[*Miss Foxhill comes out silently on rubber-soled white oxfords, and waits to be noticed. She carries a water glass.*]

Next? India, China! —In the Himalayas— [*Notices Miss Foxhill.*] What? Oh, elixir of—ha! —Isn't it kind of the drugstore to keep me alive! [*Tosses down medicine with a wry face and dismisses Miss Foxhill with a slight gesture.*] Where was I?

DOCTOR: In the Himalayas.

MRS. VENABLE: Oh yes, that long-ago summer. . . . In the Himalayas he almost entered a Buddhist monastery, had gone so far as to shave his head and eat just rice out of a wood bowl on a grass mat. He'd promised those sly Buddhist monks that he would give up the world and himself and all his worldly possessions to their mendicant order. —Well, I cabled his father, "For God's sake notify bank to freeze Sebastian's accounts!"—I got back this cable from my late husband's lawyer: "Mr. Venable critically ill Stop Wants you Stop Needs you Stop Immediate return advised most strongly. Stop. Cable time of arrival. . . ."

DOCTOR: Did you go back to your husband?

MRS. VENABLE: I made the hardest decision of my life. I stayed with my son. I got him through that crisis too. In less than a month he got up off the filthy grass mat and threw the rice bowl away— and booked us into Shepheard's Hotel in Cairo and the Ritz in Paris— And from then on, oh, we—still lived in a—world of light and shadow. . . . [*She turns vaguely with empty glass. He rises and takes it from her.*] But the shadow was almost as luminous as the light.

DOCTOR: Don't you want to sit down now?

MRS. VENABLE: Yes, indeed I do, before I fall down. [*He assists her into wheelchair.*] —Are your hindlegs still on you?

DOCTOR [*still concerned over her agitation*]: —My what? Oh—hind legs! —Yes . . .

MRS. VENABLE: Well, then you're not a donkey, you're certainly not a donkey because I've been talking the hindlegs off a donkey— several donkeys. . . . But I had to make it clear to you that the world lost a great deal too when I lost my son last summer. . . .

You would have liked my son, he would have been charmed by you. My son, Sebastian, was not a family snob or a money snob but he was a snob, all right. He was a snob about personal charm in people, he insisted upon good looks in people around him, and, oh, he had a perfect little court of young and beautiful people around him always, wherever he was, here in New *Orleans* or New York or on the Riviera or in Paris and Venice, he always had a little entourage of the beautiful and the talented and the young!

DOCTOR: Your son was young, Mrs. Venable?

MRS. VENABLE: Both of us were young, and stayed young, Doctor.

DOCTOR: Could I see a photograph of your son, Mrs. Venable?

MRS. VENABLE: Yes, indeed you could, Doctor. I'm glad that you asked to see one. I'm going to show you not one photograph but two. Here. Here is my son, Sebastian, in a Renaissance pageboy's costume at a masked ball in Cannes. Here is my son, Sebastian, in the same costume at a masked ball in Venice. These two pictures were taken twenty years apart. Now which is the older one, Doctor?

DOCTOR: This photograph looks older.

MRS. VENABLE: The photograph looks older but not the subject It takes character to refuse to grow old, Doctor—successfully to refuse to. It calls for discipline, abstention. One cocktail before dinner, not two, four, six—a single lean chop and lime juice on a salad in restaurants famed for rich dishes.

[*Foxhill comes from the house.*]

MISS FOXHILL: Mrs. Venable, Miss Holly's mother and brother are—

[*Simultaneously Mrs. Holly and George appear in the window.*]

GEORGE: Hi, Aunt Vi!

MRS. HOLLY: Violet, dear, we're here.

MISS FOXHILL: They're here.

MRS. VENABLE: Wait upstairs in my upstairs living room for me. [*To Miss Foxhill:*] Get them upstairs. I don't want them at that window during this talk. [*To the Doctor:*] Let's get away from the window. [*He wheels her to stage center.*]

DOCTOR: Mrs. Venable? Did your son have a—well—what kind of a *personal,* well, *private* life did—

MRS. VENABLE: That's a question I wanted you to ask me.

DOCTOR: Why?

MRS. VENABLE: I haven't heard the girl's story except indirectly in a watered-down version, being too ill to go to hear it directly, but I've gathered enough to know that it's a hideous attack on my son's moral character which, being dead, he can't defend himself from. I have to be the defender. Now. Sit down. Listen to me . . .

[*The Doctor sits.*]

. . . before you hear whatever you're going to hear from the girl when she gets here. My son, Sebastian, was chaste. Not c-h-a-s-e-d! Oh, he was chased in that way of spelling it, too, we had to be very fleet-footed I can tell you, with his looks and his charm, to keep ahead of pursuers, every kind of pursuer! —I mean he was c-h-a-s-t-e! —Chaste. . . .

DOCTOR: I understood what you meant, Mrs. Venable.

MRS. VENABLE: And you *believe* me, don't you?

DOCTOR: Yes, but—

MRS. VENABLE: But *what?*

DOCTOR: Chastity at—what age was your son last summer?

MRS. VENABLE: *Forty,* maybe. We really didn't count birthdays. . . .

DOCTOR: He lived a celibate life?

MRS. VENABLE: As strictly as if he'd *vowed* to! This sounds like vanity, Doctor, but really I was actually the only one in his life that satisfied the demands he made of people. Time after time my son would let people go, dismiss them!—because their, their, their!— *attitude* toward him was—

DOCTOR: Not as pure as—

MRS. VENABLE: My son, Sebastian, demanded! We were a famous couple. People didn't speak of Sebastian and his mother or Mrs. Venable and her son, they said "Sebastian and Violet, Violet and Sebastian are staying at the Lido, they're at the Ritz in Madrid. Sebastian and Violet, Violet and Sebastian have taken a house at Biarritz for the season," and every appearance, every time we appeared, attention was centered on *us!—everyone else! Eclipsed!* Vanity? Ohhhh, no, Doctor, you can't call it that—

DOCTOR: I didn't call it that.

MRS. VENABLE: —It wasn't *folie de grandeur*, it was grandeur.

DOCTOR: I see.

MRS. VENABLE: An attitude toward life that's hardly been known in the world since the great Renaissance princes were crowded out of their palaces and gardens by successful shopkeepers!

DOCTOR: I see.

MRS. VENABLE: Most people's lives—what are they but trails

of debris, each day more debris, more debris, long, long trails of debris with nothing to clean it all up but, finally, death. . . . [*We hear lyric music.*] My son, Sebastian, and I constructed our days, each day, we would—carve out each day of our lives like a piece of sculpture. —Yes, we left behind us a trail of days like a gallery of sculpture! But, last summer— [*Pause: the music continues.*] I can't forgive him for it, not even now that he's paid for it with his life! —he let in this—*vandal*! This—

DOCTOR: The girl that—?

MRS. VENABLE: That you're going to meet here this afternoon! Yes. He admitted this vandal and with her tongue for a hatchet she's gone about smashing our legend, the memory of—

DOCTOR: Mrs. Venable, what do you think is her reason?

MRS. VENABLE: Lunatics don't have reason!

DOCTOR: I mean what do you think is her—motive?

MRS. VENABLE: What a question! —We put the bread in her mouth and the clothes on her back. People that like you for that or even forgive you for it are, are—*hen's teeth,* Doctor. The role of the benefactor is worse than thankless, it's the role of a victim, Doctor, a sacrificial victim, yes, they want your blood, Doctor, they want your blood on the altar steps of their *outraged, outrageous* egos!

DOCTOR: Oh. You mean she resented the—

MRS. VENABLE: Loathed! —They can't shut her up at St. Mary's.

DOCTOR: I thought she'd been there for months.

MRS. VENABLE: I mean keep her *still* there. She *babbles*! They couldn't shut her up in Cabeza de Lobo or at the clinic in Paris— she babbled, babbled! —smashing my son's reputation. —On the

Berengaria bringing her back to the States she broke out of the stateroom and babbled, babbled; even at the airport when she was flown down here, she babbled a bit of her story before they could whisk her into an ambulance to St. Mary's. This is a reticule, Doctor. [*She raises a cloth bag.*] A catchall, carryall bag for an elderly lady which I turned into last summer. . . . Will you open it for me, my hands are stiff, and fish out some cigarettes and a cigarette holder.

[*He does.*]

DOCTOR: I don't have matches.

MRS. VENABLE: I think there's a table-lighter on the table.

DOCTOR: Yes, there is. [*He lights it, it flames up high.*] My Lord, what a torch!

MRS. VENABLE [*with a sudden, sweet smile*]: "So shines a good deed in a naughty world," Doctor—Sugar. . . .

[*Pause. A bird sings sweetly in the garden.*]

DOCTOR: Mrs. Venable?

MRS. VENABLE: Yes?

DOCTOR: In your letter last week you made some reference to a, to a—fund of some kind, an endowment fund of—

MRS. VENABLE: I wrote you that my lawyers and bankers and certified public accountants were setting up the Sebastian Venable Memorial Foundation to subsidize the work of young people like you that are pushing out the frontiers of art and science but have a financial problem. You have a financial problem, don't you, Doctor?

DOCTOR: Yes, we do have that problem. My work is such a *new* and *radical* thing that people in charge of state funds are naturally a little scared of it and keep us on a small budget, so small that—. We need a separate ward for my patients, I need trained assistants, I'd like to marry a girl I can't afford to marry! —But there's also the problem of getting right patients, not just—criminal psychopaths that the state turns over to us for my operation! —because it's—well—risky. . . . I don't want to turn you against my work at Lion's View but I have to be honest with you. There is a good deal of risk in my operation. Whenever you enter the brain with a foreign object . . .

MRS. VENABLE: Yes.

DOCTOR: —Even a needle-thin knife . . .

MRS. VENABLE: Yes.

DOCTOR: —In a skilled surgeon's fingers . . .

MRS. VENABLE: Yes.

DOCTOR: —There is a good deal of risk involved in—the operation. . . .

MRS. VENABLE: You said that it pacifies them, it quiets them down, it suddenly makes them peaceful.

DOCTOR: Yes. It does that, that much we already know, but—

MRS. VENABLE: What?

DOCTOR: Well, it will be ten years before we can tell if the immediate benefits of the operation will be lasting or—passing or even if there'd still be—and this is what haunts me about it!—any possibility, afterwards, of—reconstructing a—totally sound person, it may be that the person will always be limited afterwards, relieved of acute disturbances but—*limited,* Mrs. Venable. . . .

MRS. VENABLE: Oh, but what a blessing to them, Doctor, to be just peaceful, to be just suddenly—peaceful. . . .

[*A bird sings sweetly in the garden.*]

After all that horror, after those nightmares: just to be able to lift up their eyes and see— [*She looks up and raises a hand to indicate the sky.*] —a sky not as black with savage, devouring birds as the sky that we saw in the Encantadas, Doctor.

DOCTOR: —Mrs. Venable? I can't guarantee that a lobotomy would stop her—*babbling*!!

MRS. VENABLE: That may be, maybe not, but after the operation, who would *believe* her, Doctor?

[*Pause: faint jungle music.*]

DOCTOR [*quietly*]: My God. [*Pause.*] —Mrs. Venable, suppose after meeting the girl and observing the girl and hearing this story she babbles—I still shouldn't feel that her condition's—intractable enough! to justify the risks of—suppose I shouldn't feel that nonsurgical treatment such as insulin shock and electric shock and—

MRS. VENABLE: SHE'S HAD ALL THAT AT SAINT MARY'S!! Nothing else is left for her.

DOCTOR: But if I disagreed with you? [*Pause.*]

MRS. VENABLE: That's just part of a question: finish the question, Doctor.

DOCTOR: Would you still be interested in my work at Lion's View? I mean would the Sebastian Venable Memorial Foundation still be interested in it?

MRS. VENABLE: Aren't we always more interested in a thing that concerns us personally, Doctor?

DOCTOR: Mrs. Venable!!

[*Catharine Holly appears between the lace window curtains.*]

You're such an innocent person that it doesn't occur to you, it obviously hasn't even occurred to you that anybody less innocent than you are could possibly interpret this offer of a subsidy as— well, as sort of a *bribe*?

MRS. VENABLE [*laughs, throwing her head back*]: Name it that—I don't care—. There's just two things to remember. She's a destroyer. My son was a *creator*! —Now if my honesty's shocked you—pick up your little black bag without the subsidy in it, and run away from this garden! —Nobody's heard our conversation but you and I, Doctor Sugar. . . .

[*Miss Foxhill comes out of the house and calls.*]

MISS FOXHILL: Mrs. Venable?

MRS. VENABLE: What is it, what do you want, Miss Foxhill?

MISS FOXHILL: Mrs. Venable? Miss Holly is here, with—

[*Mrs. Venable sees Catharine at the window.*]

MRS. VENABLE: Oh, my God. There she is, in the window! —I told you I didn't want her to enter my house again, I told you to meet them at the door and lead them around the side of the house to the garden and you didn't listen. I'm not ready to face her. I have to have my five o'clock cocktail first, to fortify me. Take my chair inside. Doctor? Are you still here? I thought you'd run out of the garden. I'm going back through the garden to the other entrance. Doctor? Sugar? You may stay in the garden if you wish to or run out of the garden if you wish to or go in this way if you wish to or do anything that you wish to but I'm going to have my five o'clock daiquiri, *frozen*! —before I face her. . . .

[*All during this she has been sailing very slowly off through the garden like a stately vessel at sea with a fair wind in her sails, a pirate's frigate or a treasure-laden galleon. The young Doctor stares at Catharine framed by the lace window curtains. Sister Felicity appears beside her and draws her away from the window. Music: an ominous fanfare. Sister Felicity holds the door open for Catharine as the Doctor starts quickly forward. He starts to pick up his bag but doesn't. Catharine rushes out, they almost collide with each other.*]

CATHARINE: *Excuse me.*

DOCTOR: *I'm sorry. . . .*

[*She looks after him as he goes into the house.*]

SISTER: Sit down and be still till your family come outside.

DIM OUT

Catharine removes a cigarette from a lacquered box on the table and lights it. The following quick, cadenced lines are accompanied by quick, dancelike movement, almost formal, as the Sister in her sweeping white habit, which should be starched to make a crackling sound, pursues the girl about the white wicker patio table and among the wicker chairs: this can be accompanied by quick music.

SISTER: What did you take out of that box on the table?

CATHARINE: Just a cigarette, Sister.

SISTER: Put it back in the box.

CATHARINE: Too late, it's already lighted.

SISTER: Give it here.

CATHARINE: Oh, please, let me smoke, Sister!

SISTER: Give it here.

CATHARINE: *Please,* Sister Felicity.

SISTER: Catharine, give it here. You know that you're not allowed to smoke at Saint Mary's.

CATHARINE: We're not at Saint Mary's, this is an afternoon out.

SISTER: You're still in my charge. I can't permit you to smoke because the last time you smoked you dropped a lighted cigarette on your dress and started a fire.

CATHARINE: Oh, I did not start a fire. I just burned a hole in my skirt because I was half unconscious under medication. [*She is now back of a white wicker chair.*]

SISTER [*overlapping her*]: Catharine, give it here.

154

CATHARINE: Don't be such a bully!

SISTER: Disobedience has to be paid for later.

CATHARINE: All right, I'll pay for it later.

SISTER [*overlapping*]: Give me that cigarette or I'll make a report that'll put you right back on the violent ward, if you don't. [*She claps her hands twice and holds one hand out across the table.*]

CATHARINE [*overlapping*]: I'm not being violent, Sister.

SISTER [*overlapping*]: Give me that cigarette, I'm holding my hand out for it!

CATHARINE: All right, take it, here, take it!

[*She thrusts the lighted end of the cigarette into the palm of the Sister's hand. The Sister cries out and sucks her burned hand.*]

SISTER: *You burned me with it!*

CATHARINE: I'm sorry, I didn't mean to.

SISTER [*shocked, hurt*]: You deliberately burned me!

CATHARINE [*overlapping*]: You said give it to you and so I gave it to you.

SISTER [*overlapping*]: You stuck the lighted end of that cigarette in my hand!

CATHARINE [*overlapping*]: I'm *sick*, I'm *sick*! —of being *bossed* and *bullied*!

SISTER [*commandingly*]: *Sit down!*

[*Catharine sits down stiffly in a white wicker chair on forestage, facing the audience. The Sister resumes sucking the burned*

155

palm of her hand. Ten beats. Then from inside the house the whirr of a mechanical mixer.]

CATHARINE: There goes the Waring Mixer, Aunt Violet's about to have her five o'clock frozen daiquiri, you could set a watch by it! [*She almost laughs. Then she draws a deep, shuddering breath and leans back in her chair, but her hands remain clenched on the white wicker arms.*] —We're in Sebastian's garden. *My God, I can still cry!*

SISTER: Did you have any medication before you went out?

CATHARINE: No. I didn't have any. Will you give me some, Sister?

SISTER [*almost gently*]: I can't. I wasn't told to. However, I think the doctor will give you something.

CATHARINE: The young blond man I bumped into?

SISTER: Yes. The young doctor's a specialist from another hospital.

CATHARINE: What hospital?

SISTER: A word to the wise is sufficient. . . .

[*The Doctor has appeared in the window.*]

CATHARINE [*rising abruptly*]: I knew I was being watched, he's in the window, staring out at me!

SISTER: Sit down and be still. Your family's coming outside.

CATHARINE [*overlapping*]: LION'S VIEW, IS IT! DOCTOR?

[*She has advanced toward the bay window, The Doctor draws back, letting the misty white gauze curtains down to obscure him.*]

SISTER [*rising with a restraining gesture which is almost pity-ing*]: Sit down, dear.

CATHARINE: IS IT LION'S VIEW? DOCTOR?!

SISTER: Be still. . . .

CATHARINE: WHEN CAN I STOP RUNNING DOWN THAT STEEP WHITE STREET IN CABEZA DE LOBO?

SISTER: Catharine, dear, sit down.

CATHARINE: I loved him, Sister! Why wouldn't he let me save him? I tried to hold onto his hand but he struck me away and ran, ran, ran in the wrong direction, Sister!

SISTER: Catharine, dear—be still. [*The Sister sneezes.*]

CATHARINE: Bless you, Sister. [*She says this absently, still watching the window.*]

SISTER: Thank you.

CATHARINE: The Doctor's still at the window but he's too blond to hide behind window curtains, he catches the light, he shines through them. [*She turns from the window.*] —We were *going* to blonds, blonds were next on the menu.

SISTER: Be still now. Quiet, dear.

CATHARINE: Cousin Sebastian said he was famished for blonds, he was fed up with the dark ones and was famished for blonds. All the travel brochures he picked up were advertisements of the blond northern countries. I think he'd already booked us to— Copenhagen or—Stockholm. —Fed up with dark ones, famished for light ones: that's how he talked about people, as if they were— items on a menu. —"That one's delicious-looking, that one is ap-petizing," or "that one is *not* appetizing"—I think because he was really nearly half-starved from living on pills and salads. . . .

SISTER: *Stop it!* —Catharine, be still.

CATHARINE: He liked me and so I loved him. . . . [*She cries a little again.*] If he'd kept hold of my hand I could have saved him! —Sebastian suddenly said to me last summer: "Let's fly north, little bird—I want to walk under those radiant, cold northern lights—I've never *seen* the aurora borealis!"—Somebody said once or wrote, once: "We're all of us children in a vast kindergarten trying to spell God's name with the wrong alphabet blocks!"

MRS. HOLLY [*offstage*]: *Sister?*

[*The Sister rises.*]

CATHARINE [*rising*]: I think it's *me* they're calling, they call *me* "Sister," Sister!

The Sister resumes her seat impassively as the girl's mother and younger brother appear from the garden. The mother, Mrs. Holly, is a fatuous Southern lady who requires no other description. The brother, George, is typically good looking, he has the best "looks" of the family, tall and elegant of figure. They enter.

MRS. HOLLY: Catharine, dear! Catharine— [*They embrace tentatively.*] Well, well! Doesn't she look fine, George?

GEORGE: Uh huh.

CATHARINE: They send you to the beauty parlor whenever you're going to have a family visit. Other times you look awful, you can't have a compact or lipstick or anything made out of metal because they're afraid you'll swallow it.

MRS. HOLLY [*giving a tinkly little laugh*]: I think she looks just splendid, don't you, George?

GEORGE: Can't we talk to her without the nun for a minute?

MRS. HOLLY: Yes, I'm sure it's all right to. Sister?

CATHARINE: Excuse me, Sister Felicity, this is my mother, Mrs. Holly, and my brother, George.

SISTER: How do you do.

GEORGE: How d'ya do.

CATHARINE: This is Sister Felicity. . . .

MRS. HOLLY: We're so happy that Catharine's at Saint Mary's! So very grateful for all you're doing for her.

SISTER [*sadly, mechanically*]: We do the best we can for her, Mrs. Holly.

MRS. HOLLY: I'm sure you do. Yes, well—I wonder if you would mind if we had a little private chat with our Cathie?

SISTER: I'm not supposed to let her out of my sight.

MRS. HOLLY: It's just for a minute. You can sit in the hall or the garden and we'll call you right back here the minute the private part of the little talk is over.

[*Sister Felicity withdraws with an uncertain nod and a swish of starched fabric.*]

GEORGE [*to Catharine*]: *Jesus! What are you up to? Huh? Sister? Are you trying to RUIN us?!*

MRS. HOLLY: GAWGE! WILL YOU BE QUIET. You're upsetting your sister!

[*He jumps up and stalks off a little, rapping his knee with his zipper-covered tennis racket.*]

CATHARINE: How elegant George looks.

MRS. HOLLY: George inherited Cousin Sebastian's wardrobe but everything else is in probate! Did you know that? That everything else is in probate and Violet can keep it in probate just as long as she wants to?

CATHARINE: Where is Aunt Violet?

MRS. HOLLY: *George, come back here!*

[*He does, sulkily.*]

Violet's on her way down.

GEORGE: Yeah. Aunt Violet has an elevator now.

MRS. HOLLY: Yais, she has, she's had an elevator installed where the back stairs were, and, Sister, it's the cutest little thing you ever did see! It's paneled in Chinese lacquer, black an' gold Chinese lacquer, with lovely bird-pictures on it. But there's only room for two people at a time in it. George and I came down on foot—I think she's havin' her frozen daiquiri now, she still has a frozen daiquiri promptly at five o'clock ev'ry afternoon in the world . . . in warm weather. . . . Sister, the horrible death of Sebastian just about *killed* her! —She's now slightly better . . . but it's a question of time. —Dear, you know, I'm sure that you understand, why we haven't been out to see you at Saint Mary's. They said you were too disturbed, and a family visit might disturb you more. But I want you to know that nobody, absolutely nobody in the city, knows a thing about what you've been through. Have they, George? Not a thing. Not a soul even knows that you've come back from Europe. When people enquire, when they question us about you, we just say that you've stayed abroad to study something or other. [*She catches her breath.*] Now. Sister? —I want you to please be *very* careful what you say to your Aunt Violet about what happened to Sebastian in Cabeza de Lobo.

CATHARINE: What do you want me to say about what—?

MRS. HOLLY: Just don't repeat that same fantastic story! For my sake and George's sake, the sake of your brother and mother, don't repeat that horrible story again! Not to Violet! Will you?

CATHARINE: Then I am going to have to tell Aunt Violet what happened to her son in Cabeza de Lobo?

MRS. HOLLY: Honey, that's why you're here. She has *INSISTED* on hearing it straight from YOU!

GEORGE: You were the only witness to it, Cathie.

CATHARINE: No, there were others. That *ran.*

MRS. HOLLY: Oh, Sister, you've just had a little sort of a—*nightmare* about it! Now, listen to me, will you, Sister? Sebastian has left, has BEQUEATHED! —to you an' Gawge in his *will*—

GEORGE [*religiously*]: *To each of us, fifty grand, each!* —
AFTER! TAXES! —GET IT?

CATHARINE: Oh, yes, but if they give me an injection—I won't
have any choice but to tell exactly what happened in Cabeza de
Lobo last summer. Don't you see? I won't have any choice but to
tell the truth. It makes you tell the truth because it shuts something
off that might make you able not to and *everything* comes out,
decent or *not* decent, you have no control, but always, always the
truth!

MRS. HOLLY: Catharine, darling. I don't know the full story,
but surely you're not too sick in your *head* to know in your *heart*
that the story you've been telling is just—too—

GEORGE [*cutting in*]: Cathie, Cathie, you got to forget that
story! Can'tcha? For *your* fifty grand?

MRS. HOLLY: Because if Aunt Vi contests the will, and we know
she'll contest it, she'll keep it in the courts forever! —We'll be—

GEORGE: It's in PROBATE NOW! And'll never get out of probate until you drop that story—we can't afford to hire lawyers
good enough to contest it! So if you don't stop telling that crazy
story, we won't have a pot to—cook *greens* in!

[*He turns away with a fierce grimace and a sharp, abrupt wave
of his hand, as if slapping down something. Catharine stares at
his tall back for a moment and laughs wildly.*]

MRS. HOLLY: Catharine, don't laugh like that, it scares me,
Catharine.

[*Jungle birds scream in the garden.*]

GEORGE [*turning his back on his sister*]: Cathie, the money is
all tied up.

[*He stoops over sofa, hands on flannel knees, speaking directly into Catharine's face as if she were hard of hearing. She raises a hand to touch his cheek affectionately; he seizes the hand and removes it but holds it tight.*]

If Aunt Vi decided to contest Sebastian's will that leaves us all of this cash?! —Am I coming through to you?

CATHARINE: Yes, little brother, you are.

GEORGE: You see, Mama, she's crazy like a coyote! [*He gives her a quick cold kiss.*] We won't get a single damn penny, honest t' God we won't! So you've just GOT to stop tellin' that story about what you say happened to Cousin Sebastian in Cabeza de Lobo, even if it's what it *couldn't* be, TRUE! —You got to drop it, Sister, you can't tell such a story to civilized people in a civilized up-to-date country!

MRS. HOLLY: Cathie, why, why, why! —did you invent such a tale?

CATHARINE: But, Mother, I DIDN'T invent it. I know it's a hideous story but it's a true story of our time and the world we live in and what did truly happen to Cousin Sebastian in Cabeza de Lobo. . . .

GEORGE: Oh, then you are going to tell it. Mama, she IS going to tell it! Right to Aunt Vi, and lose us a hundred thousand! — Cathie? You are a BITCH!

MRS. HOLLY: GAWGE!

GEORGE: I repeat it, a bitch! She isn't crazy, Mama, she's no more crazy than I am, she's just, just—PERVERSE! Was ALWAYS! —perverse. . . .

[*Catharine turns away and breaks into quiet sobbing.*]

MRS. HOLLY: Gawge, Gawge, apologize to Sister, this is no way for you to talk to your sister. You come right back over here and tell your sweet little sister you're sorry you spoke like that to her!

GEORGE [*turning back to Catharine*]: I'm sorry, Cathie, but you know we NEED that money! Mama and me, we—Cathie? I got *ambitions*! And, Cathie, I'm YOUNG! —I *want* things, I *need* them, Cathie! So will you please think about ME? Us?

MISS FOXHILL [*off stage*]: Mrs. Holly? Mrs. Holly?

MRS. HOLLY: Somebody's callin' fo' me. Catharine, Gawge put it very badly but you know that it's TRUE! WE DO HAVE TO GET WHAT SEBASTIAN HAS LEFT US IN HIS WILL, DEAREST! AND YOU WON'T LET US DOWN? PROMISE? YOU WON'T? LET US DOWN?

GEORGE [*fiercely shouting*]: HERE COMES AUNT VI! Mama, Cathie, Aunt Violet's—here is Aunt Vi!

Mrs. Venable enters downstage area. Entrance music.

MRS. HOLLY: *Cathie! Here's Aunt Vi!*

MRS. VENABLE: She sees me and I see her. That's all that's necessary. Miss Foxhill, put my chair in this corner. Crank the back up a little.

[*Miss Foxhill does this business.*]

More. More. Not that much! —Let it back down a little. All right. Now, then. I'll have my frozen daiquiri, now. . . . Do any of you want coffee?

GEORGE: I'd like a chocolate malt.

MRS. HOLLY: Gawge!

MRS. VENABLE: This isn't a drugstore.

MRS. HOLLY: Oh, Gawge is just being Gawge.

MRS. VENABLE: That's what I *thought* he was being!

[*An uncomfortable silence falls. Miss Foxhill creeps out like a burglar. She speaks in a breathless whisper, presenting a cardboard folder toward Mrs. Venable.*]

MISS FOXHILL: Here's the portfolio marked Cabeza de Lobo. It has all your correspondence with the police there and the American consul.

MRS. VENABLE: I asked for the *English transcript*! It's in a separate—

MISS FOXHILL: Separate, yes, here it is!

MRS. VENABLE: Oh . . .

MISS FOXHILL: And here's the report of the private investigators and here's the report of—

MRS. VENABLE: Yes, yes, yes! Where's the doctor?

MISS FOXHILL: On the phone in the library!

MRS. VENABLE: Why does he choose such a moment to make a phone call?

MISS FOXHILL: He didn't make a phone call, he received a phone call from—

MRS. VENABLE: Miss Foxhill, why are you talking to me like a burglar!?

[*Miss Foxhill giggles a little desperately.*]

CATHARINE: Aunt Violet, she's frightened. —Can I move? Can I get up and move around till it starts?

MRS. HOLLY: Cathie, Cathie, dear, did Gawge tell you that he received bids from every good fraternity on the Tulane campus and went Phi Delt because Paul Junior did?

MRS. VENABLE: I see that he had the natural tact and good taste to come here this afternoon outfitted from head to foot in clothes that belonged to my son!

GEORGE: You gave 'em to me, Aunt Vi.

MRS. VENABLE: I didn't know you'd parade them in front of me, George.

MRS. HOLLY [*quickly*]: Gawge, tell Aunt Violet how grateful you are for—

GEORGE: I found a little Jew tailor on Britannia Street that makes alterations so good you'd never guess that they weren't cut *out* for me to *begin* with!

MRS. HOLLY: *AND* so reasonable! —Luckily, since it seems that Sebastian's wonderful, wonderful bequest to Gawge an' Cathie is going to be tied up a while!?

GEORGE: Aunt Vi? About the will?

[*Mrs. Holly coughs.*]

I was just wondering if we can't figure out some way to, to—

MRS. HOLLY: Gawge means to EXPEDITE it! To get through the red tape quicker?

MRS. VENABLE: I understand his meaning. Foxhill, get the Doctor.

[*She has risen with her cane and hobbled to the door.*]

MISS FOXHILL [*exits calling*]: Doctor!

MRS. HOLLY: Gawge, no more about money.

GEORGE: How do we know we'll ever see her again?

[*Catharine gasps and rises; she moves downstage, followed quickly by Sister Felicity.*]

SISTER [*mechanically*]: What's wrong, dear?

CATHARINE: I think I'm just dreaming this, it doesn't seem real!

[*Miss Foxhill comes back out, saying:*]

MISS FOXHILL: He had to answer an urgent call from Lion's View.

[*Slight, tense pause.*]

MRS. HOLLY: Violet! *Not* Lion's View!

[*Sister Felicity had started conducting Catharine back to the patio; she stops her, now.*]

SISTER: Wait, dear.

CATHARINE: What for? I know what's coming.

MRS. VENABLE [*at same time*]: Why? Are you all prepared to put out a thousand a month plus extra charges for treatments to keep the girl at St. Mary's?

MRS. HOLLY: Cathie? Cathie, dear?

[*Catharine has returned with the Sister.*]

Tell Aunt Violet how grateful you are for her makin' it possible for you to rest an' recuperate at such a sweet, sweet place as St. Mary's!

CATHARINE: No place for lunatics is a sweet, sweet place.

MRS. HOLLY: But the food's good there. Isn't the food good there?

CATHARINE: Just give me written permission not to eat fried grits. I had yard privileges till I refused to eat fried grits.

SISTER: She lost yard privileges because she couldn't be trusted in the yard without constant supervision or even with it because she'd run to the fence and make signs to cars on the highway.

CATHARINE: Yes, I did, I did that because I've been trying for weeks to get a message out of that "sweet, sweet place."

MRS. HOLLY: What message, dear?

CATHARINE: I got panicky, Mother.

MRS. HOLLY: Sister, I don't understand.

GEORGE: What're you scared of, Sister?

CATHARINE: What they might do to me now, after they've done

all the rest! —That man in the window's a specialist from Lion's View! We get newspapers. I know what they're . . .

[*The Doctor comes out.*]

MRS. VENABLE: Why, Doctor, I thought you'd left us with just that little black bag to remember you by!

DOCTOR: Oh, no. Don't you remember our talk? I had to answer a call about a patient that—

MRS. VENABLE: This is Dr. Cukrowicz. He says it means "sugar" and we can call him "Sugar"—

[*George laughs.*]

He's a specialist from Lion's View.

CATHARINE [*cutting in*]: WHAT DOES HE SPECIALIZE IN?

MRS. VENABLE: Something new. When other treatments have failed.

[*Pause. The jungle clamor comes up and subsides again.*]

CATHARINE: *Do you want to bore a hole in my skull and turn a knife in my brain?* Everything else was done to me!

[*Mrs. Holly sobs. George raps his knee with the tennis racket.*]

You'd have to have my mother's permission for that.

MRS. VENABLE: I'm paying to keep you in a private asylum.

CATHARINE: You're not my legal guardian.

MRS. VENABLE: Your mother's dependent on me. All of you are! —Financially. . . .

CATHARINE: I think the situation is—clear to me, now. . . .

MRS. VENABLE: Good! In that case. . . .

DOCTOR: I think a quiet atmosphere will get us the best results.

MRS. VENABLE: I don't know what you mean by a quiet atmosphere. She shouted, I didn't.

DOCTOR: Mrs. Venable, let's try to keep things on a quiet level, now. Your niece seems to be disturbed.

MRS. VENABLE: She has every reason to be. She took my son from me, and then she—

CATHARINE: Aunt Violet, you're not being fair.

MRS. VENABLE: Oh, aren't I?

CATHARINE [to the others]: She's not being fair. [Then back to Mrs. Venable:] Aunt Violet, you know why Sebastian asked me to travel with him.

MRS. VENABLE: Yes, I do know why!

CATHARINE: You weren't able to travel. You'd had a— [She stops short.]

MRS. VENABLE: Go on! What had I had? Are you afraid to say it in front of the Doctor? She meant that I had a stroke. —I DID NOT HAVE A STROKE! —I had a slight aneurism. You know what that is, Doctor? A little vascular convulsion! Not a hemorrhage, just a little convulsion of a blood vessel. I had it when I discovered that she was trying to take my son away from me. Then I had it. It gave a little temporary—muscular—contraction. —To one side of my face. . . . [She crosses back into main acting area.] These people are not blood relatives of mine, they're my dead husband's relations. I always detested these people, my dead husband's sister and—her two worthless children. But I did more than my duty to keep their heads above water. To please my son, whose weakness was being excessively softhearted, I went to the expense and humiliation, yes, public humiliation, of giving this girl a debut which was a fiasco. Nobody liked her when I brought her out. Oh, she had some kind of—notoriety! She had a sharp tongue that some people mistook for wit. A habit of laughing in the faces of decent people which would infuriate them, and also reflected adversely on me and Sebastian, too. But, he, Sebastian, was amused by this girl. While I was disgusted, sickened. And halfway through the season, she was dropped off the party lists, yes, dropped off the lists in spite of my position. Why? Because she'd lost her head over a young married man, made a scandalous scene at a Mardi Gras ball, in the middle of the ballroom. Then everybody dropped her like a hot—rock, but— [*She loses her breath.*] My son, Sebastian, still felt sorry for her and took her with him last summer instead of me. . . .

CATHARINE [*springing up with a cry*]: I can't change truth, I'm not God! I'm not even sure that He could, I don't think God can change truth! How can I change the story of what happened to her son in Cabeza de Lobo?

MRS. VENABLE [*at the same time*]: She was in love with my son!

CATHARINE [*overlapping*]: Let me go back to Saint Mary's. Sister Felicity, let's go back to Saint—

MRS. VENABLE [*overlapping*]: Oh, no! That's not where you'll go!

CATHARINE [*overlapping*]: All right, *Lion's View* but don't ask me to—

MRS. VENABLE [*overlapping*]: You *know* that you were!

CATHARINE [*overlapping*]: That I was *what*, Aunt Violet?

MRS. VENABLE [*overlapping*]: Don't call me "Aunt," you're the niece of my dead husband, not me!

MRS. HOLLY [*overlapping*]: Catharine, Catharine, don't upset your—Doctor? Oh, Doctor!

[*But the Doctor is calmly observing the scene, with detachment. The jungle-garden is loud with the sounds of its feathered and scaled inhabitants.*]

CATHARINE: I don't want to, I didn't want to come here! I know what she thinks, she thinks I murdered her son, she thinks that I was responsible for his death.

MRS. VENABLE: That's right. I told him when he told me that he was going with you in my place last summer that I'd never see him again and I never did. And only you know why!

CATHARINE: Oh, my God, I—

[*She rushes out toward garden, followed immediately by the Sister.*]

SISTER: Miss Catharine, Miss Catharine—

DOCTOR [*overlapping*]: Mrs. Venable?

SISTER [*overlapping*]: Miss Catharine?

DOCTOR [*overlapping*]: Mrs. Venable?

MRS. VENABLE: What?

DOCTOR: I'd like to be left alone with Miss Catharine for a few minutes.

MRS. HOLLY: George, talk to her, George.

[*George crouches appealingly before the old lady's chair, peering close into her face, a hand on her knee.*]

GEORGE: Aunt Vi? Cathie can't go to Lion's View. Everyone in the Garden District would know you'd put your niece in a state asylum, Aunt Vi.

MRS. VENABLE: Foxhill!

GEORGE: What do you want, Aunt Vi?

MRS. VENABLE: Let go of my chair. Foxhill? Get me away from these people!

GEORGE: Aunt Vi, listen, think of the talk it—

MRS. VENABLE: I can't get up! Push me, push me away!

GEORGE [*rising but holding chair*]: I'll push her, Miss Foxhill.

MRS. VENABLE: Let go of my chair or—

MISS FOXHILL: Mr. Holly, I—

GEORGE: I got to talk to her.

[*He pushes her chair downstage.*]

MRS. VENABLE: Foxhill!

MISS FOXHILL: Mr. Holly, she doesn't want you to push her.

GEORGE: I know what I'm doing, leave me alone with Aunt Vi!

MRS. VENABLE: Let go me or I'll *strike* you!

GEORGE: Oh, Aunt Vi!

MRS. VENABLE: Foxhill!

MRS. HOLLY: George—

GEORGE: Aunt Vi?

[*She strikes at him with her cane. He releases the chair and Miss Foxhill pushes her off. He trots after her a few steps, then he returns to Mrs. Holly, who is sobbing into a handkerchief. He sighs, and sits down beside her, taking her hand. The scene fades as light is brought up on Catharine and the Sister in the garden. The Doctor comes up to them. Mrs. Holly stretches her arms out to George, sobbing, and he crouches before her chair and rests his head in her lap. She strokes his head. During this: the Sister has stood beside Catharine, holding onto her arm.*]

CATHARINE: You don't have to hold onto me. I can't run away.

DOCTOR: Miss Catharine?

CATHARINE: What?

DOCTOR: Your aunt is a very sick woman. She had a stroke last spring?

CATHARINE: Yes, she did, but she'll never admit it . . .

DOCTOR: You have to understand why.

CATHARINE: I do, I understand why. I didn't want to come here.

DOCTOR: Miss Catharine, do you hate her?

CATHARINE: I don't understand what hate is. How can you hate anybody and still be sane? You see, I still think I'm sane!

DOCTOR: You think she did have a stroke?

CATHARINE: She had a slight stroke in April. It just affected one side, the left side, of her face . . . but it was disfiguring, and after that, Sebastian couldn't use her.

DOCTOR: Use her? Did you say use her?

[*The sounds of the jungle-garden are not loud but ominous.*]

CATHARINE: Yes, we all use each other and that's what we think of as love, and not being able to use each other is what's—*hate.* . . .

DOCTOR: Do you hate her, Miss Catharine?

CATHARINE: Didn't you ask me that, once? And didn't I say that I didn't understand hate. A ship struck an iceberg at sea—everyone sinking—

DOCTOR: Go on, Miss Catharine!

CATHARINE: But that's no reason for everyone drowning for hating everyone drowning! Is it, Doctor?

DOCTOR: Tell me: what was your feeling for your cousin Sebastian?

CATHARINE: He liked me and so I loved him.

DOCTOR: In what way did you love him?

CATHARINE: The only way he'd accept: —a sort of motherly way. I tried to save him, Doctor.

DOCTOR: From what? Save him from what?

CATHARINE: Completing! —a sort of! —*image*! —he had of himself as a sort of! —*sacrifice* to a! —*terrible* sort of a—

DOCTOR: —God?

CATHARINE: Yes, a—*cruel* one, Doctor!

DOCTOR: How did you feel about that?

CATHARINE: Doctor, my feelings are the sort of feelings that you have in a dream. . . .

DOCTOR: Your life doesn't seem real to you?

CATHARINE: Suddenly last winter I began to write my journal in the third person.

[*He grasps her elbow and leads her out upon forestage. At the same time Miss Foxhill wheels Mrs. Venable off, Mrs. Holly weeps into a handkerchief and George rises and shrugs and turns his back to the audience.*]

DOCTOR: Something happened last winter?

CATHARINE: At a Mardi Gras ball some—some boy that took me to it got too drunk to stand up! [*A short, mirthless note of laughter.*] I wanted to go home. My coat was in the cloakroom, they couldn't find the check for it in his pockets. I said, "Oh, hell, let it go!"—I started out for a taxi. Somebody took my arm and said, "I'll drive you home." He took off his coat as we left the hotel and put it over my shoulders, and then I looked at him and—I don't think I'd ever even seen him before then, really! — He took me home in his car but took me another place first. We stopped near the Duelling Oaks at the end of Esplanade Street. . . . Stopped! —I said, "What for?"—He didn't answer, just struck a match in the car to light a cigarette in the car and I looked at him in the car and I knew "what for"! —I think I got out of the car before he got out of the car, and we walked through the wet grass to the great misty oaks as if somebody was calling us for help there!

[*Pause. The subdued, toneless bird-cries in the garden turn to a single bird song.*]

DOCTOR: After that?

CATHARINE: I lost him. —He took me home and said an awful thing to me. "We'd better forget it," he said, "my wife's expecting a child and—"—I just entered the house and sat there thinking a little and then I suddenly called a taxi and went right back to the Roosevelt Hotel ballroom. The ball was still going on. I thought I'd gone back to pick up my borrowed coat but that wasn't what I'd gone back for. I'd gone back to make a scene on the floor of the ballroom, yes, I didn't stop at the cloakroom to pick up Aunt Violet's old mink stole, no, I rushed right into the ballroom and spotted him on the floor and ran up to him and beat him as hard as I could in the face and chest with my fists till—Cousin Sebastian took me away. —After that, the next morning, I started writing my diary in the third person, singular, such as "She's still living this morning," meaning that *I* was. . . . —"WHAT'S NEXT FOR HER? GOD KNOWS!"—I couldn't go out any more. —However one morning my Cousin Sebastian came in my bedroom and said: "Get up!"—Well . . . if you're still alive after dying, well then, you're obedient, Doctor. —I got up. He took me downtown to a place for passport photos. Said: "Mother can't go abroad with me this summer. You're going to go with me this summer instead of Mother."—If you don't believe me, read my journal of Paris! —"She woke up at daybreak this morning, had her coffee and dressed and took a brief walk—"

DOCTOR: *Who* did?

CATHARINE: *She* did. *I* did—from the Hotel Plaza Athénée to the Place de l'Etoile as if pursued by a pack of Siberian wolves! [*She laughs her tired, helpless laugh.*] —Went right through all stop signs—couldn't wait for green signals. —"Where did she think she was going? Back to the Duelling Oaks?"—Everything chilly and dim but his hot, ravenous mouth! on—

DOCTOR: Miss Catharine, let me give you something.

[*The others go out, leaving Catharine and the Doctor onstage.*]

CATHARINE: Do I have to have the injection again, this time? What am I going to be stuck with this time, Doctor? I don't care. I've been stuck so often that if you connected me with a garden hose I'd make a good sprinkler.

DOCTOR [*preparing needle*]: Please take off your jacket.

[*She does. The Doctor gives her an injection.*]

CATHARINE: I didn't feel it.

DOCTOR: That's good. Now sit down.

[*She sits down.*]

CATHARINE: Shall I start counting backwards from a hundred?

DOCTOR: Do you like counting backwards?

CATHARINE: Love it! Just love it! One hundred! Ninety-nine! Ninety-eight! Ninety-seven. Ninety-six. Ninety—five— Oh! —I already feel it! How funny!

DOCTOR: That's right. Close your eyes for a minute.

[*He moves his chair closer to hers. Half a minute passes.*]

Miss Catharine? I want you to give me something.

CATHARINE: Name it and it's yours, Doctor Sugar.

DOCTOR: Give me all your resistance.

CATHARINE: Resistance to what?

DOCTOR: The truth. Which you're going to tell me.

CATHARINE: The truth's the one thing I have never resisted!

DOCTOR: Sometimes people just think they don't resist it, but still do.

CATHARINE: They say it's at the bottom of a bottomless well, you know.

DOCTOR: Relax.

CATHARINE: Truth.

DOCTOR: Don't talk.

CATHARINE: Where was I, now? At ninety?

DOCTOR: You don't have to count backwards.

CATHARINE: At ninety something?

DOCTOR: You can open your eyes.

CATHARINE: Oh, I do feel funny!

[*Silence, pause.*]

You know what I think you're doing? I think you're trying to hypnotize me. Aren't you? You're looking so straight at me and doing something to me with your eyes and your—eyes. . . . Is that what you're doing to me?

DOCTOR: Is that what you *feel* I'm doing?

CATHARINE: Yes! I feel so peculiar. And it's not just the drug.

DOCTOR: Give me all your resistance. See. I'm holding my hand out. I want you to put yours in mine and give me all your resistance. Pass all of your resistance out of your hand to mine.

CATHARINE: Here's my hand. But there's no resistance in it.

DOCTOR: You are totally passive.

CATHARINE: Yes, I am.

DOCTOR: You will do what I ask.

CATHARINE: Yes, I will try.

DOCTOR: You will tell the true story.

CATHARINE: Yes, I will.

DOCTOR: The absolutely true story. No lies, nothing not spoken. Everything told, exactly.

CATHARINE: Everything. Exactly. Because I'll have to. Can I—can I stand up?

DOCTOR: Yes, but be careful. You might feel a little bit dizzy.

[*She struggles to rise, then falls back.*]

CATHARINE: I can't get up! Tell me to. Then I think I could do it.

DOCTOR: Stand up.

[*She rises unsteadily.*]

CATHARINE: How funny! Now I can! Oh, I do feel dizzy! Help me, I'm—

[*He rushes to support her.*]

—about to fall over. . . .

[*He holds her. She looks out vaguely toward the brilliant, steaming garden. Looks back at him. Suddenly sways toward him, against him.*]

DOCTOR: You see, you lost your balance.

CATHARINE: No, I didn't. I did what I wanted to do without you telling me to. [*She holds him tight against her.*] Let me! Let! Let! Let me! Let me, let me, oh, let me. . . .

[*She crushes her mouth to his violently. He tries to disengage himself. She presses her lips to his fiercely, clutching his body against her. Her brother George enters.*]

Please hold me! I've been so lonely. It's lonelier than death, if I've gone mad, it's lonelier than death!

GEORGE [*shocked, disgusted*]: *Cathie!* —you've got a hell of a nerve.

[*She falls back, panting, covers her face, runs a few paces and grabs the back of a chair. Mrs. Holly enters.*]

MRS. HOLLY: What's the matter, George? Is Catharine ill?

GEORGE: No.

DOCTOR: Miss Catharine had an injection that made her a little unsteady.

MRS. HOLLY: What did he say about Catharine?

[*Catharine has gone out into the dazzling jungle of the garden.*]

SISTER [*returning*]: She's gone into the garden.

DOCTOR: That's all right, she'll come back when I call her.

SISTER: It may be all right for you. You're not responsible for her.

[*Mrs. Venable has reentered.*]

MRS. VENABLE: Call her now!

DOCTOR: Miss Catharine! Come back. [*To the Sister:*] Bring her back, please, Sister!

[*Catharine enters quietly, a little unsteady.*]

Now, Miss Catharine, you're going to tell the true story.

CATHARINE: Where do I start the story?

DOCTOR: Wherever you think it started.

CATHARINE: I think it started the day he was born in this house.

MRS. VENABLE: Ha! You see!

GEORGE: Cathie.

DOCTOR: Let's start later than that. [*Pause.*] Shall we begin with last summer?

CATHARINE: Oh. Last summer.

DOCTOR: Yes. Last summer.

[*There is a long pause. The raucous sounds in the garden fade into a bird song which is clear and sweet. Mrs. Holly coughs. Mrs. Venable stirs impatiently. George crosses downstage to catch Catharine's eye as he lights a cigarette.*]

CATHARINE: Could I—?

MRS. VENABLE: Keep that boy away from her!

GEORGE: She wants to smoke, Aunt Vi.

CATHARINE: Something helps in the—hands. . . .

SISTER: Unh unh!

DOCTOR: It's all right, Sister. [*He lights her cigarette.*] About last summer: how did it begin?

CATHARINE: It began with his kindness and the six days at sea that took me so far away from the—Duelling Oaks that I forgot them, nearly. He was affectionate with me, so sweet and attentive to me, that some people took us for a honeymoon couple until they noticed that we had—separate staterooms, and—then in Paris, he took me to Patou and Schiaparelli's—*this* is from Schiaparelli's! [*Like a child, she indicates her suit.*] —bought me so many new clothes that I gave away my old ones to make room for my new ones in my new luggage to—travel. . . . I turned into a peacock! Of course, so was *he* one, too. . . .

GEORGE: *Ha ha!*

MRS. VENABLE: Shh!

CATHARINE: But then I made the mistake of responding too much to his kindness, of taking hold of his hand before he'd take hold of mine, of holding onto his arm and leaning on his shoulder, of appreciating his kindness more than he wanted me to, and, suddenly, last summer, he began to be restless, and—oh!

DOCTOR: Go on.

CATHARINE: The Blue Jay notebook!

DOCTOR: Did you say notebook?

MRS. VENABLE: I know what she means by that, she's talking about the school composition book with a Blue Jay trademark that Sebastian used for making notes and revisions on his *Poem of Summer.* It went with him everywhere that he went, in his jacket pocket, even his dinner jacket. I have the one that he had with him last summer. *Foxhill! The Blue Jay notebook!*

[*Miss Foxhill rushes in with a gasp.*]

It came with his personal effects shipped back from Cabeza de Lobo.

DOCTOR: I don't quite get the connection between new clothes and so forth and the Blue Jay notebook.

MRS. VENABLE: I HAVE IT! —Doctor, tell her I've found it.

[*Miss Foxhill hears this as she comes back out of house: gasps with relief, retires.*]

DOCTOR: With all these interruptions it's going to be awfully hard to—

MRS. VENABLE: This is important. I don't know why she mentioned the Blue Jay notebook but I want you to see it. Here it is, here! [*She holds up a notebook and leafs swiftly through the pages.*] Title? *Poem of Summer,* and the date of the summer— 1935. After that: *what? Blank pages, blank pages,* nothing but *nothing!* —last summer. . . .

DOCTOR: What's that got to do with—?

MRS. VENABLE: His destruction? I'll tell you. A poet's vocation is something that rests on something as thin and fine as the web of a spider, Doctor. That's all that holds him *over*! —out of destruction. . . . Few, very few are able to do it alone! Great help is needed! I *did* give it! She *didn't*.

CATHARINE: She's right about that. I failed him. I wasn't able to keep the web from—breaking. . . . I saw it breaking but couldn't save or—repair it!

MRS. VENABLE: There now, the truth's coming out. We had an agreement between us, a sort of contract or covenant between us which he broke last summer when he broke away from me and took her with him, not me! When he was frightened and I knew when and what of, because his hands would shake and his eyes looked in, not out, I'd reach across a table and touch his hands and say not a word, just look, and touch his hands with my hand until his hands stopped shaking and his eyes looked out, not in, and in the morning, the poem would be continued. *Continued until it was finished!*

[*The following ten speeches are said very rapidly, overlapping.*]

CATHARINE: I—couldn't!

MRS. VENABLE: *Naturally* not! He was *mine*! I *knew* how to help him, I *could*! You didn't, you couldn't!

DOCTOR: These interruptions—

MRS. VENABLE: I would say "You *will*" and he *would*, I—!

CATHARINE: Yes, you see, I failed him! And so, last summer, we went to Cabeza de Lobo, we flew down there from where he gave up writing his poem last summer. . . .

MRS. VENABLE: Because he'd broken our—

CATHARINE: Yes! Yes, something had broken, that string of pearls that old mothers hold their sons by like a—sort of a—sort of—*umbilical* cord, *long—after* . . .

MRS. VENABLE: She means that I held him back from—

DOCTOR: *Please!*

MRS. VENABLE: *Destruction!*

CATHARINE: All I know is that suddenly, last summer, he wasn't young any more, and we went to Cabeza de Lobo, and he suddenly switched from the evenings to the beach. . . .

DOCTOR: From evenings? To beach?

CATHARINE: I mean from the evenings to the afternoons and from the fa—fash—

[*Silence. Mrs. Holly draws a long, long painful breath. George stirs impatiently.*]

DOCTOR: Fashionable! Is that the word you—?

CATHARINE: Yes. Suddenly, last summer Cousin Sebastian changed to the afternoons and the beach.

DOCTOR: What beach?

CATHARINE: In Cabeza de Lobo there is a beach that's named for Sebastian's name saint, it's known as La Playa San Sebastian, and that's where we started spending all afternoon, every day.

DOCTOR: What kind of beach was it?

CATHARINE: It was a big city beach near the harbor.

DOCTOR: It was a big public beach?

CATHARINE: Yes, public.

MRS. VENABLE: It's little statements like that that give her away.

[*The Doctor rises and crosses to Mrs. Venable without breaking his concentration on Catharine.*]

After all I've told you about his fastidiousness, can you accept such a statement?

DOCTOR: You mustn't interrupt her.

MRS. VENABLE [*overlapping him*]: That Sebastian would go every day to some dirty free public beach near a harbor? A man that had to go out a mile in a boat to find water fit to swim in?

DOCTOR: Mrs. Venable, no matter what she says you have to let her say it without any more interruptions or this interview will be useless.

MRS. VENABLE: I won't speak again. I'll keep still, if it kills me.

CATHARINE: I don't want to go on. . . .

DOCTOR: Go on with the story. Every afternoon last summer your Cousin Sebastian and you went out to this free public beach?

CATHARINE: No, it wasn't the free one, the free one was right next to it, there was a fence between the free beach and the one that we went to that charged a small charge of admission.

DOCTOR: Yes, and what did you do there?

[*He still stands beside Mrs. Venable and the light gradually changes as the girl gets deeper into her story: the light concentrates on Catharine, the other figures sink into shadow.*]

Did anything happen there that disturbed you about it?

CATHARINE: Yes!

DOCTOR: What?

CATHARINE: He bought me a swimsuit I didn't want to wear. I laughed. I said, "I can't wear that, it's a scandal to the jay birds!"

DOCTOR: What did you mean by that? That the suit was immodest?

CATHARINE: My God, yes! It was a one-piece suit made of white lisle, the water made it transparent! [*She laughs sadly at the memory of it.*] —I didn't want to swim in it, but he'd grab my hand and drag me into the water, all the way in, and I'd come out looking naked!

DOCTOR: Why did he do that? Did you understand why?

CATHARINE: —Yes! To attract! —Attention.

DOCTOR: He wanted you to attract attention, did he, because he felt you were moody? Lonely? He wanted to shock you out of your depression last summer?

CATHARINE: Don't you understand? I was PROCURING for him!

[*Mrs. Venable's gasp is like the sound that a great hooked fish might make.*]

She used to do it, *too*.

[*Mrs. Venable cries out.*]

Not consciously! She didn't *know* that she was procuring for him in the smart, the fashionable places they used to go to before last summer! Sebastian was shy with people. She wasn't. Neither was I. We both did the same thing for him, made contacts for him, but she did it in nice places and in decent ways and I had to do it the way that I just told you! —Sebastian was lonely, Doctor, and the empty Blue Jay notebook got bigger and bigger, so big it was big and empty as that big empty blue sea and sky. . . . I knew what I was doing. I came out in the French Quarter years before I came out in the Garden District. . . .

MRS. HOLLY: Oh, Cathie! Sister . . .

DOCTOR: Hush!

CATHARINE: And before long, when the weather got warmer and the beach so crowded, he didn't need me any more for that purpose. The ones on the free beach began to climb over the fence or swim around it, bands of homeless young people that lived on the free beach like scavenger dogs, hungry children. . . . So now he let me wear a decent dark suit. I'd go to a faraway empty end of the beach, write postcards and letters and keep up my— third-person journal till it was—five o'clock and time to meet him outside the bathhouses, on the street. . . . He would come out, *followed*.

DOCTOR: Who would follow him out?

CATHARINE: The homeless, hungry young people that had climbed over the fence from the free beach that they lived on. He'd pass out tips among them as if they'd all—shined his shoes or called taxis for him. . . . Each day the crowd was bigger, noisier, greedier! —Sebastian began to be frightened. —At last we stopped going out there. . . .

DOCTOR: And then? After that? After you quit going out to the public beach?

CATHARINE: Then one day, a few days after we stopped going out to the beach—it was one of those white blazing days in Cabeza de Lobo, not a blazing hot *blue* one but a blazing hot *white* one.

DOCTOR: Yes?

CATHARINE: We had a late lunch at one of those open-air restaurants on the sea there—Sebastian was white as the weather. He had on a spotless white silk Shantung suit and a white silk tie and a white panama and white shoes, white—white lizard skin—pumps! He— [*She throws back her head in a startled laugh at the recollection.*] —kept touching his face and his throat here and there with a white silk handkerchief and popping little white pills in his mouth, and I knew he was having a bad time with his heart and was frightened about it and that was the reason we hadn't gone out to the beach. . . .

[*During the monologue the lights have changed, the surrounding area has dimmed out and a hot white spot is focused on Catharine.*]

"I think we ought to go north," he kept saying, "I think we've done Cabeza de Lobo, I think we've done it, don't you?" *I* thought we'd done it! —but I had learned it was better not to seem to have an opinion because if I did, well, Sebastian, well, you know Sebastian, he always preferred to do what no one else wanted to do, and I always tried to give the impression that I was agreeing reluctantly to his wishes . . . it was a—game. . . .

SISTER: She's dropped her cigarette.

DOCTOR: I've got it, Sister.

[*There are whispers, various movements in the penumbra. The Doctor fills a glass for her from the cocktail shaker.*]

CATHARINE: Where was I? Oh, yes, that five o'clock lunch at one of those fish places along the harbor of Cabeza de Lobo, it was between the city and the sea, and there were naked children along the beach which was fenced off with barbed wire from the restaurant and we had our table less than a yard from the barbed wire fence that held the beggars at bay. . . . There were naked children along the beach, a band of frightfully thin and dark naked children that looked like a flock of plucked birds, and they would come darting up to the barbed wire fence as if blown there by the wind, the hot white wind from the sea, all crying out, "*Pan, pan, pan!*"

DOCTOR [*quietly*]: What's *pan?*

CATHARINE: The word for bread, and they made gobbling noises with their little black mouths, stuffing their little black fists to their mouths and making those gobbling noises, with frightful grins! —Of course we were sorry that we had come to this place but it was too late to go. . . .

DOCTOR [*quietly*]: Why was it "too late to go"?

CATHARINE: I told you Cousin Sebastian wasn't well. He was popping those little white pills in his mouth. I think he had popped in so many of them that they had made him feel weak. . . . His, his! —eyes looked—dazed, but he said: "Don't look at those little monsters. Beggars are a social disease in this country. If you look at them, you get sick of the country, it spoils the whole country for you. . . ."

DOCTOR: Go on.

CATHARINE: I'm going on. I have to wait now and then till it gets clearer. Under the drug it has to be a vision, or nothing comes. . . .

DOCTOR: All right?

CATHARINE: Always when I was with him I did what he told me. I didn't look at the band of naked children, not even when the waiters drove them away from the barbed wire fence with sticks! —Rushing out through a wicket gate like an assault party in war! —and beating them screaming away from the barbed wire fence with the sticks. . . . Then! [*Pause.*]

DOCTOR: Go on, Miss Catherine, what comes next in the vision?

CATHARINE: The, the, the! —band of children began to— serenade us. . . .

DOCTOR: Do what?

CATHARINE: Play for us! On instruments! Make music! —if you could call it music. . . .

DOCTOR: Oh?

CATHARINE: Their, their—instruments were—instruments of percussion! —Do you know what I mean?

DOCTOR [*making a note*]: Yes. Instruments of percussion such as—*drums?*

CATHARINE: I stole glances at them when Cousin Sebastian wasn't looking, and as well as I could make out in the white blaze of the sand-beach, the instruments were tin cans strung together.

DOCTOR [*slowly, writing*]: *Tin—cans—strung—together.*

CATHARINE: *And, and, and, and—and! —bits of metal, other* bits of metal that had been flattened out, made into—

DOCTOR: What?

CATHARINE: *Cymbals!* You know? *Cymbals?*

DOCTOR: Yes. Brass plates hit together.

CATHARINE: That's right, Doctor. —Tin cans flattened out and clashed together! —Cymbals. . . .

DOCTOR: Yes. I understand. What's after that, in the vision?

CATHARINE [*rapidly, panting a little*]: And others had paper

191

bags, bags made out of—coarse paper!—with something on a string inside the bags which they pulled up and down, back and forth, to make a sort of a—

DOCTOR: Sort of a—?

CATHARINE: Noise like—

DOCTOR: Noise like?

CATHARINE [*rising stiffly from chair*]: Ooompa! Oompa! Oooooompa!

DOCTOR: Ahhh . . . a sound like a *tuba*?

CATHARINE: That's right!—they made a sound like a tuba. . . .

DOCTOR: Oompa, oompa, oompa, like a tuba.

[*He is making a note of the description.*]

CATHARINE: Oompa, oompa, oompa, like a—

[*Short pause.*]

DOCTOR: —Tuba. . . .

CATHARINE: All during lunch they stayed at a—a fairly *close—distance.* . . .

DOCTOR: Go on with the vision, Miss Catharine.

CATHARINE [*striding about the table*]: *Oh, I'm going on, nothing could stop it now!!*

DOCTOR: Your Cousin Sebastian was *entertained* by this —concert?

CATHARINE: I think he was *terrified* of it!

DOCTOR: Why was he terrified of it?

CATHARINE: I think he recognized some of the musicians, some of the boys, between childhood and—older. . . .

DOCTOR: What did he do? Did he do anything about it, Miss Catharine? —Did he complain to the manager about it?

CATHARINE: *What* manager? *God*? Oh, *no!* —The manager of the fish place on the beach? Haha! —No! —You don't understand my cousin!

DOCTOR: What do you mean?

CATHARINE: *He!* —*accepted!* —*all!* —as—how! —things! —are! —And thought nobody had any right to complain or interfere in any way whatsoever, and even though he knew that what was awful was awful, that what was wrong was wrong, and my Cousin Sebastian was certainly never sure that anything was wrong! —He thought it unfitting to ever take any action about anything whatsoever! —except to go on doing as something in him directed. . . .

DOCTOR: What did something in him direct him to do? —I mean on this occasion in Cabeza de Lobo.

CATHARINE: After the salad, before they brought the coffee, he suddenly pushed himself away from the table, and said, "They've got to stop that! Waiter, make them stop that. I'm not a well man, I have a heart condition, it's making me sick!" —This was the first time that Cousin Sebastian had ever attempted to correct a human situation! —I think perhaps that *that* was his—fatal error. . . . It was then that the waiters, all eight or ten of them, charged out of the barbed wire wicket gate and beat the little musicians away with clubs and skillets and anything hard that they could snatch from the kitchen! —Cousin Sebastian left the table. He stalked out of the restaurant after throwing a handful of paper money on the table and he fled from the place. I followed. It was all white outside. White hot, a blazing white hot, hot blazing white, at five o'clock in the afternoon in the city of—Cabeza de Lobo. It looked as if—

DOCTOR: It looked as if?

CATHARINE: As if a huge white bone had caught on fire in the sky and blazed so bright it was white and turned the sky and everything under the sky white with it!

DOCTOR: —White . . .

CATHARINE: Yes—white . . .

DOCTOR: You followed your Cousin Sebastian out of the restaurant onto the hot white street?

CATHARINE: Running up and down hill. . . .

DOCTOR: You ran up and down hill?

CATHARINE: No, no! *Didn't*—move either *way*! —at first, we were—

[*During this recitation there are various sound effects. The percussive sounds described are very softly employed.*]

I rarely made any suggestion but *this* time I *did*. . . .

DOCTOR: What did you suggest?

CATHARINE: Cousin Sebastian seemed to be paralyzed near the entrance of the café, so I said, "Let's go." I remember that it was a very wide and steep white street, and I said, "Cousin Sebastian, down that way is the waterfront and we are more likely to find a taxi near there. . . . Or why don't we go back in? —and have them *call* us a taxi! Oh, let's do! Let's do *that*, that's better!" And he said, "*Mad*, are you *mad*? Go back in that filthy place? Never! That gang of kids shouted vile things about me to the waiters!" "Oh," I said, "then let's go down toward the docks, down there at

194

the bottom of the hill, let's not try to climb the hill in this dreadful heat." And Cousin Sebastian shouted, "Please shut up, let me handle this situation, will you? I want to handle this thing." And he started up the steep street with a hand stuck in his jacket where I knew he was having a pain in his chest from his palpitations. . . . But he walked faster and faster, in panic, but the faster he walked the louder and closer it got!

DOCTOR: What got louder?

CATHARINE: The music.

DOCTOR: The music again.

CATHARINE: The oompa-oompa of the—following band. —They'd somehow gotten through the barbed wire and out on the street, and they were following, following! —up the blazing white street. The band of naked children pursued us up the steep white street in the sun that was like a great white bone of a giant beast that had caught on fire in the sky! —Sebastian started to run and they all screamed at once and seemed to fly in the air, they outran him so quickly. I screamed. I heard Sebastian scream, he screamed just once before this flock of black plucked little birds that pursued him and overtook him halfway up the white hill.

DOCTOR: And you, Miss Catharine, what did *you* do, then?

CATHARINE: Ran!

DOCTOR: Ran where?

CATHARINE: Down! Oh, I ran down, the easier direction to run was down, down, down, down! —The hot, white, blazing street, screaming out "Help" all the way, till—

DOCTOR: What?

CATHARINE: —Waiters, police, and others—ran out of buildings and rushed back up the hill with me. When we got back to where my Cousin Sebastian had disappeared in the flock of featherless little black sparrows, he—he was lying naked as they had been naked against a white wall, and this you won't believe, nobody *has* believed it, nobody *could* believe it, nobody, nobody on earth could possibly believe it, and I don't *blame* them! —They had *devoured* parts of him.

[*Mrs. Venable cries out softly.*]

Torn or cut parts of him away with their hands or knives or maybe those jagged tin cans they made music with, they had torn bits of him away and stuffed them into those gobbling fierce little empty black mouths of theirs. There wasn't a sound any more, there was nothing to see but Sebastian, what was left of him, that looked like a big white-paper-wrapped bunch of red roses had been *torn, thrown, crushed!* —against that blazing white wall . . .

[*Mrs. Venable springs with amazing power from her wheelchair, stumbles erratically but swiftly toward the girl and tries to strike her with her cane. The Doctor snatches it from her and catches her as she is about to fall. She gasps hoarsely several times as he leads her toward the exit.*]

MRS. VENABLE [*off stage*]: Lion's View! State asylum, cut this hideous story out of her brain!

[*Mrs. Holly sobs and crosses to George, who turns away from her, saying:*]

GEORGE: Mom, I'll quit school, I'll get a job, I'll—

MRS. HOLLY: Hush son! Doctor, can't you say something?

[*Pause. The Doctor comes downstage. Catharine wanders out into the garden followed by the Sister.*]

DOCTOR [*after a while, reflectively, into space*]: I think we ought at least to consider the possibility that the girl's story could be true. . . .

THE END

THE PAST, THE PRESENT,
AND THE PERHAPS

One icy bright winter morning in the last week of 1940, my brave representative, Audrey Wood, and I were crossing the Common in Boston, from an undistinguished hotel on one side to the grandeur of the Ritz-Carlton on the other. We had just read the morning notices of *Battle of Angels,* which had opened at the Wilbur the evening before. As we crossed the Common there was a series of loud reports like gunfire from the street that we were approaching, and one of us said, "My God, they're shooting at us!"

We were still laughing, a bit hysterically, as we entered the Ritz-Carlton suite in which the big brass of the Theatre Guild and director Margaret Webster were waiting for us with that special air of gentle gravity that hangs over the demise of a play so much like the atmosphere that hangs over a home from which a living soul has been snatched by the Reaper.

Not present was little Miriam Hopkins, who was understandably shattered and cloistered after the events of the evening before, in which a simulated on-stage fire had erupted clouds of smoke so realistically over both stage and auditorium that a lot of Theatre

Guild first-nighters had fled choking from the Wilbur before the choking star took her bows, which were about the quickest and most distracted that I have seen in a theater.

It was not that morning that I was informed that the show must close. That morning I was only told that the play must be cut to the bone. I came with a rewrite of the final scene and I remember saying, heroically, "I will crawl on my belly through brimstone if you will substitute this." The response was gently evasive. It was a few mornings later that I received the *coup de grace,* the announcement that the play would close at the completion of its run in Boston. On that occasion I made an equally dramatic statement, on a note of anguish. "You don't seem to see that I put my heart into this play!"

It was Miss Webster who answered with a remark I have never forgotten and yet never heeded. She said, "You must not wear your heart on your sleeve for daws to peck at!" Someone else said, "At least you are not out of pocket." I don't think I had any answer for that one, any more than I had anything in my pocket to be out of.

Well, in the end, when the Boston run was finished, I was given a check for $200 and told to get off somewhere and rewrite the play. I squandered half of this subsidy on the first of four operations performed on a cataracted left eye, and the other half took me to Key West for the rewrite. It was a long rewrite. In fact, it is still going on, though the two hundred bucks are long gone.

Why have I stuck so stubbornly to this play? For seventeen years, in fact? Well, nothing is more precious to anybody than the emotional record of his youth, and you will find the trail of my sleeve-worn heart in this completed play that I now call *Orpheus Descending.* On its surface it was and still is the tale of a wild-spirited boy who wanders into a conventional community of the South and creates the commotion of a fox in a chicken coop.

But beneath that now familiar surface, it is a play about unanswered questions that haunt the hearts of people and the difference between continuing to ask them, a difference represented by the four major protagonists of the play, and the acceptance of prescribed answers that are not answers at all, but expedient adaptations or surrender to a state of quandary.

Battle was actually my fifth long play, but the first to be given a professional production. Two of the others, *Candles to the Sun* and *Fugitive Kind,* were produced by a brilliant, but semiprofessional group called The Mummers of St. Louis. A third one, called *Spring Storm,* was written for the late Prof. E. C. Mabie's seminar in playwriting at the University of Iowa, and I read it aloud, appropriately in the spring.

When I had finished reading, the good professor's eyes had a glassy look as though he had drifted into a state of trance. There was a long and all but unendurable silence. Everyone seemed more or less embarrassed. At last the professor pushed back his chair, thus dismissing the seminar, and remarked casually and kindly, "Well, we all have to paint our nudes!" And this is the only reference that I can remember anyone making to the play. That is, in the playwriting class, but I do remember that the late Lemuel Ayers, who was a graduate student at Iowa that year, read it and gave me sufficient praise for its dialogue and atmosphere to reverse my decision to give up the theater in favor of my other occupation of waiting on tables, or more precisely, handing out trays in the cafeteria of the State Hospital.

Then there was Chicago for a while and a desperate effort to get on the W. P. A. Writers' Project, which didn't succeed, for my work lacked "social content" or "protest" and I couldn't prove that my family was destitute and I still had, in those days, a touch of refinement in my social behavior which made me seem frivolous and decadent to the conscientiously roughhewn pillars of the Chicago Project.

And so I drifted back to St. Louis, again, and wrote my fourth long play which was the best of the lot. It was called *Not About Nightingales* and it concerned prison life, and I have never written anything since then that could compete with it in violence and horror, for it was based on something that actually occurred along about that time, the literal roasting alive of a group of intransigent convicts sent for correction to a hot room called "The Klondike."

I submitted it to The Mummers of St. Louis and they were eager to perform it but they had come to the end of their economic tether and had to disband at this point.

Then there was New Orleans and another effort, while waiting on tables in a restaurant where meals cost only two-bits, to get on a Writers' Project or the Theatre Project, again unsuccessful.

And then there was a wild and wonderful trip to California with a young clarinet player. We ran out of gas in El Paso, also out of cash, and it seemed for days that we would never go farther, but my grandmother was an "easy touch" and I got a letter with a $10 bill stitched neatly to one of the pages, and we continued westward.

In the Los Angeles area, in the summer of 1939, I worked for a while at Clark's Bootery in Culver City, within sight of the M.G.M studio and I lived on a pigeon ranch, and I rode between the two, a distance of ten miles, on a secondhand bicycle that I bought for $5.

Then a most wonderful thing happened. While in New Orleans I had heard about a play contest being conducted by the Group Theatre of New York. I submitted all four of the long plays I have mentioned that preceded *Battle of Angels,* plus a group of one-acts called *American Blues.* One fine day I received, when I returned to the ranch on my bike, a telegram saying that I had won a special award of $100 for the one-acts, and it was signed by Harold Clurman, Molly Day Thacher, who is the present Mrs. Elia Kazan, and that fine writer, Irwin Shaw, the judges of the contest.

I retired from Clark's Bootery and from picking squabs at the pigeon ranch. And the clarinet player and I hopped on our bicycles and rode all the way down to Tijuana and back as far as Laguna Beach, where we obtained, rent free, a small cabin on a small ranch in return for taking care of the poultry.

We lived all that summer on the $100 from the Group Theatre and I think it was the happiest summer of my life. All the days were pure gold, the nights were starry, and I looked so young, or carefree, that they would sometimes refuse to sell me a drink because I did not appear to have reached twenty-one. But toward the end of the summer, maybe only because it was the end of the summer as well as the end of the $100, the clarinet player became very moody and disappeared without warning into the San Bernardino Mountains to commune with his soul in solitude, and there was nothing left in the cabin in the canyon but a bag of dried peas.

I lived on stolen eggs and avocados and dried peas for a week, and also on a faint hope stirred by a letter from a lady in New York whose name was Audrey Wood, who had taken hold of all those plays that I had submitted to the Group Theatre contest, and told me that it might be possible to get me one of the Rockefeller Fellowships, or grants, of $1,000 which were being passed out to gifted young writers at that time. And I began to write *Battle of Angels,* a lyric play about memories and the loneliness of them. Although my beloved grandmother was living on the pension of a retired minister (I believe it was only $85 a month in those days), and her meager earnings as a piano instructor, she once again stitched some bills to a page of a letter, and I took a bus to St. Louis. *Battle of Angels* was finished late that fall and sent to Miss Wood.

One day the phone rang and, in a terrified tone, my mother told me that it was long distance, for me. The voice was Audrey Wood's. Mother waited, shakily, in the doorway. When I hung up I said, quietly, "Rockefeller has given me a $1,000 grant and they want me to come to New York." For the first time since I had known her, my mother burst into tears. "I am so happy," she said. It was all she could say.

And so you see it is a very old play that *Orpheus Descending* has come out of, but a play is never an old one until you quit working on it and I have never quit working on this one, not even now. It never went into the trunk, it always stayed on the workbench, and I am not presenting it now because I have run out of ideas or material for completely new work. I am offering it this season because I honestly believe that it is finally finished. About seventy-five percent of it is new writing, but, what is much more important, I believe that I have now finally managed to say in it what I wanted to say, and I feel that it now has in it a sort of emotional bridge between those early years described in this article and my present state of existence as a playwright.

So much for the past and present. The future is called "perhaps," which is the only possible thing to call the future. And the important thing is not to allow that to scare you.

TENNESSEE WILLIAMS, 1957

A CHRONOLOGY

1907   June 3: Cornelius Coffin Williams and Edwina Estelle Dakin marry in Columbus, Mississippi.

1909   November 19: Sister, Rose Isabelle Williams, is born in Columbus, Mississippi.

1911   March 26: Thomas Lanier Williams III is born in Columbus, Mississippi.

1918   July: Williams family moves to St. Louis, Missouri.

1919   February 21: Brother, Walter Dakin Williams, is born in St. Louis, Missouri.

1928   Short story "The Vengeance of Nitocris" is published in *Weird Tales* magazine.

        July: Williams's grandfather, Walter Edwin Dakin (1857–1954), takes young Tom on a tour of Europe.

1929   September: Begins classes at the University of Missouri at Columbia.

1930   Writes the one-act play *Beauty is the Word* for a contest. at U. of M.

1932   Summer: Fails ROTC and is taken out of college by his father and put to work as a clerk at the International Shoe Company.

1936   January: Enrolls in extension courses at Washington University, St. Louis.

1937   March 18 and 20: First full-length play, *Candles to the Sun*, is produced by the Mummers theater, St. Louis.

       September: Transfers to the University of Iowa.

       November 30 and December 4: *Fugitive Kind* is performed by the Mummers.

1938   Graduates from the University of Iowa with a degree in English.

       Completes the play *Not About Nightingales*.

1939   Receives an award from the Group Theatre for a group of short plays collectively titled *American Blues*, which leads to his association with Audrey Wood, his agent for the next thirty-two years.

       Story magazine publishes "The Field of Blue Children" with the first printed use of his professional name, "Tennessee Williams."

1940   January through June: Studies playwriting with John Gassner at the New School for Social Research in New York City.

       December 30: *Battle of Angels*, starring Miriam Hopkins, suffers a disastrous first night during its out-of-town try-out in Boston and closes shortly thereafter.

1942   December: At a cocktail party in New York, meets James Laughlin, founder of New Directions, who is to become Williams' lifelong friend and publisher.

1943   January 13: A bilateral prefrontal lobotomy is performed on Rose Isabelle Williams, leaving her in a childlike mental state for the rest of her life.

       October 13: A collaboration with his friend Donald Windham, *You Touched Me!* (based on a story by D. H. Lawrence), premieres at the Cleveland Playhouse.

1944   December 26: *The Glass Menagerie* opens in Chicago star-
         ring Laurette Taylor.

         A group of poems, "The Summer Belvedere," is published
         in *Five Young American Poets, 1944*. (Books listed here
         are published by New Directions unless otherwise indi-
         cated.)

1945   March 25: *Stairs to the Roof* premieres at the Pasadena
         Playhouse in California.

         March 31: *The Glass Menagerie* opens on Broadway and
         wins the Drama Critics Circle Award for best play.

         September 25: *You Touched Me!* opens on Broadway, and
         is later published by Samuel French.

         December 27: *Wagons Full of Cotton and Other Plays* is
         published.

1947   Summer: Meets Frank Merlo (1929–1963) in Province-
         town—starting in 1948 they become lovers and compan-
         ions, and remain together for fourteen years.

         December 3: *A Streetcar Named Desire,* directed by Elia
         Kazan and starring Jessica Tandy, Marlon Brando, Kim
         Hunter, and Karl Malden, opens on Broadway and wins
         the Pulitzer Prize and the Drama Critics Circle Award.

1948   October 6: *Summer and Smoke* opens on Broadway and
         closes in just over three months.

1949   January: *One Arm and Other Stories* is published.

1950   The novel *The Roman Spring of Mrs. Stone* is published.

         The film version of *The Glass Menagerie* is released.

1951   February 3: *The Rose Tattoo* opens on Broadway starring
         Maureen Stapleton and Eli Wallach and wins the Tony
         Award for best play of the year.

The film version of *A Streetcar Named Desire* is released starring Vivian Leigh and Marlon Brando.

1952　April 24: A revival of *Summer and Smoke* directed by José Quintero and starring Geraldine Page opens off-Broadway at the Circle at the Square and is a critical success.

The National Institute of Arts and Letters inducts Williams as a member.

1953　March 19: *Camino Real* opens on Broadway and after a harsh critical reception closes within two months.

1954　A book of stories, *Hard Candy*, is published in August.

1955　March 24: *Cat on a Hot Tin Roof* opens on Broadway directed by Elia Kazan and starring Barbara Bel Geddes, Ben Gazzara and Burl Ives. *Cat* wins the Pulitzer Prize and the Drama Critics Circle Award.

The film version of *The Rose Tattoo*, for which Anna Magnani later wins an Academy Award, is released.

1956　The film *Baby Doll*, with a screenplay by Williams and directed by Elia Kazan, is released amid some controversy and is blacklisted by Catholic leader Cardinal Spellman.

June: *In the Winter of Cities*, Williams's first book of poetry, is published.

1957　March 21: *Orpheus Descending*, a revised version of *Battle of Angels*, directed by Harold Clurman, opens on Broadway but closes after two months.

1958　February 7: *Suddenly Last Summer* and *Something Unspoken* open off-Broadway under the collective title *Garden District*.

The film version of *Cat on a Hot Tin Roof* is released.

1959　March 10: *Sweet Bird of Youth* opens on Broadway and runs for three months.

The film version of *Suddenly Last Summer*, with a screenplay by Gore Vidal, is released.

1960   November 10: The comedy *Period of Adjustment* opens on Broadway and runs for over four months.

The film version of *Orpheus Descending* is released under the title *The Fugitive Kind*.

1961   December 29: *The Night of the Iguana* opens on Broadway and runs for nearly ten months.

The film versions of *Summer and Smoke* and *The Roman Spring of Mrs. Stone* are released.

1962   The film versions of *Sweet Bird of Youth* and *Period of Adjustment* are released.

1963   January 15: *The Milk Train Doesn't Stop Here Anymore* opens on Broadway and closes due to a blizzard and a newspaper strike. It is revived January 1, 1964, starring Tallulah Bankhead and Tab Hunter and closes within a week.

September: Frank Merlo dies of lung cancer.

1964   The film version of *Night of the Iguana* is released.

1966   February 22: *Slapstick Tragedy* (*The Mutilated* and *The Gnädiges Fräulein*) runs on Broadway for a week.

December: A novella and stories are published under the title *The Knightly Quest*.

1968   March 27: *Kingdom of Earth* opens on Broadway under the title *The Seven Descents of Myrtle*.

The film version of *The Milk Train Doesn't Stop Here Anymore* is released under the title *Boom!*

1969   May 11: *In the Bar of a Tokyo Hotel* opens off-Broadway and runs for three weeks.

Committed by his brother Dakin for three months to the Renard Psychiatric Division of Barnes Hospital in St. Louis.

The film version of *Kingdom of Earth* is released under the title *The Last of the Mobile Hot Shots*.

Awarded Doctor of Humanities degree by the University of Missouri and a Gold Medal for Drama by the American Academy of Arts and Letters.

1970   February: A book of plays, *Dragon Country*, is published.

1971   Williams fires his agent Audrey Wood. Bill Barnes assumes his representation, and then later Mitch Douglas.

1972   April 2: *Small Craft Warnings* opens off-Broadway.

1973   March 1: *Out Cry*, the revised version of *The Two-Character Play*, opens on Broadway.

1974   September: *Eight Mortal Ladies Possessed*, a book of short stories, is published.

Williams is presented with a Medal of Honor for Literature from the National Arts Club.

1975   The novel *Moise and the World of Reason* is published by Simon & Schuster and *Memoirs* is published by Doubleday.

1976   January 20: *This Is (An Entertainment)* opens in San Francisco at the American Conservatory Theater.

June: *The Red Devil Battery Sign* closes during its out-of-town tryout in Boston.

November 23: *Eccentricities of a Nightingale*, a rewritten version of *Summer and Smoke*, opens in New York.

April: Williams's second volume of poetry, *Androgyne, Mon Amour*, is published.

1977   May 11: *Vieux Carré* opens on Broadway and closes within two weeks.

1978   *Tiger Tail* premieres at the Alliance Theater in Atlanta, Georgia, and a revised version premieres the following year at the Hippodrome Theater in Gainsville, Florida.

1979   January 10: *A Lovely Sunday for Creve Coeur* opens off-Broadway.

       Kirche, Küche, Kinder workshops off-Broadway at the Jean Cocteau Repertory Theater.

       Williams is presented with a Lifetime Achievement Award at the Kennedy Center Honors in Washington by President Jimmy Carter.

1980   January 25: *Will Mr. Merriwether Return from Memphis?* premieres for a limited run at the Tennessee Williams Performing Arts Center in Key West, Florida.

       March 26: Williams's last Broadway play, *Clothes for a Summer Hotel*, opens and closes after two weeks.

1981   August 24: *Something Cloudy, Something Clear* premieres off-Broadway at the Jean Cocteau Repertory Theater.

1982   May 8: The final version of *A House Not Meant to Stand* opens at the Goodman Theater in Chicago.

1983   February 24: Williams is found dead in his room at the Hotel Elysee in New York City. Williams is later buried in St. Louis.

1984   July: *Stopped Rocking and Other Screenplays* is published.

1985   November: *Collected Stories*, with an introduction by Gore Vidal, is published.

1995   Lyle Leverich's biography, *Tom: The Unknown Tennessee Williams*, is published by Crown Publishers.

1996   September 5: Rose Isabelle Williams dies in Tarrytown, New York.

        September 5: *The Notebook of Trigorin*, in a revised version, opens at the Cincinnati Playhouse in the Park.

1998   March 5: *Not About Nightingales* premieres at the Royal National Theatre in London, directed by Trevor Nunn, and opens November 25, 1999, on Broadway.

1999   November: *Spring Storm* is published.

2000   May: *Stairs to the Roof* is published.

        November: *The Selected Letters of Tennessee Williams, Volume I* is published.

2001   June: *Fugitive Kind* is published.

2002   April: *Collected Poems* is published.

2004   August: *Candles to the Sun* is published.

        November: *The Selected Letters of Tennessee Williams, Volume II* is published.

2005   April: *Mister Paradise and Other One-Act Plays* is published.

2008   April: *A House Not Meant to Stand* and *The Traveling Companion and Other Plays* are published.

        May 20: (Walter) Dakin Williams dies at the age of 89 in Belleville, Illinois.

2011   April: *The Magic Tower and Other One-Act Plays* is published.